SCOOBY-DOO'S

LAUGH-OUT-LOUD JOKES!

by Michael Dahl

illustrated by Scott Jeralds

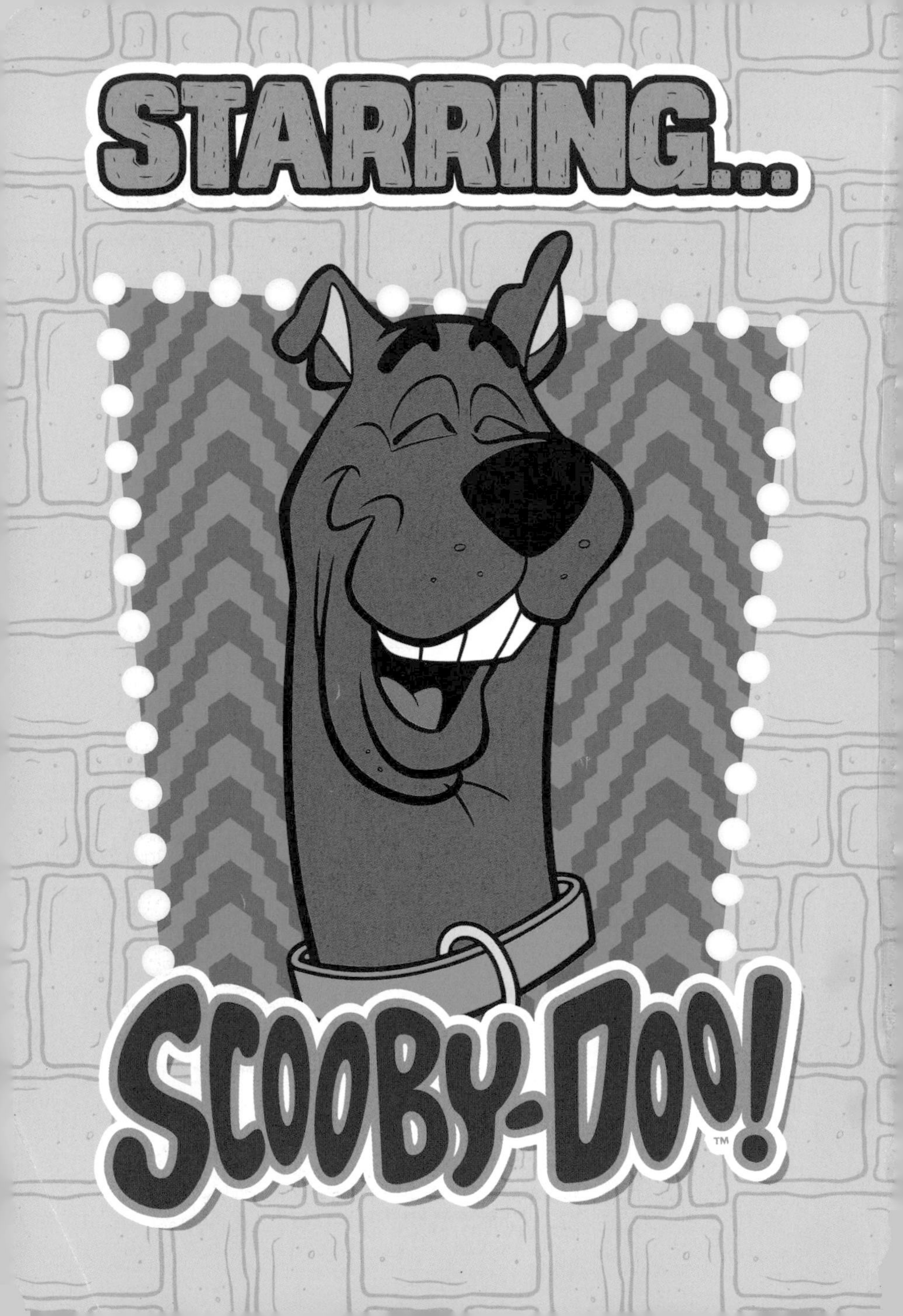
STARRING...
SCOOBY-DOO!™

Shaggy!

Velma!

Fred!

Daphne!

...AND MORE!

Published by Capstone Young Readers
A Capstone Imprint
1710 Roe Crest Drive
North Mankato, Minnesota 56003
www.capstoneyoungreaders.com

CAPS34358

Cataloging-in-Publication Data is available on the Library of Congress website.
ISBN: 978-1-62370-182-6 [paperback]
ISBN: 978-1-62370-476-6 [ebook]

Summary:
Scooby-Doo is up to some funny business . . . are you? Hop on board the Mystery
Machine and join the laughs, jokes, and fun!

Editor: Eliza Leahy
Designer: Bob Lentz
Production: Gene Bentdahl

SET LIST:

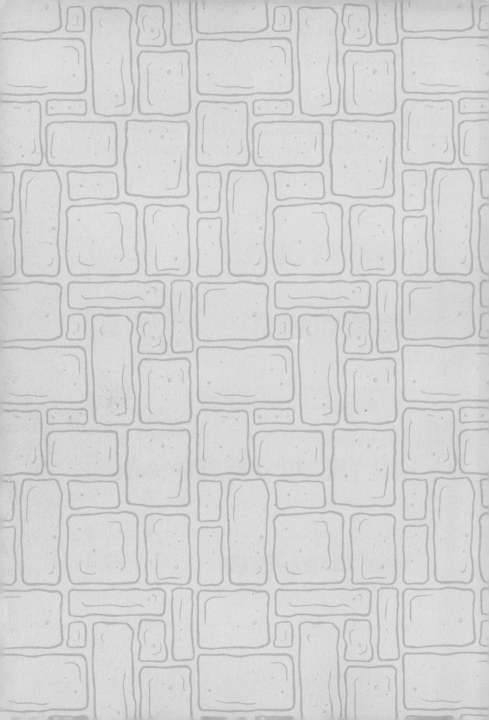

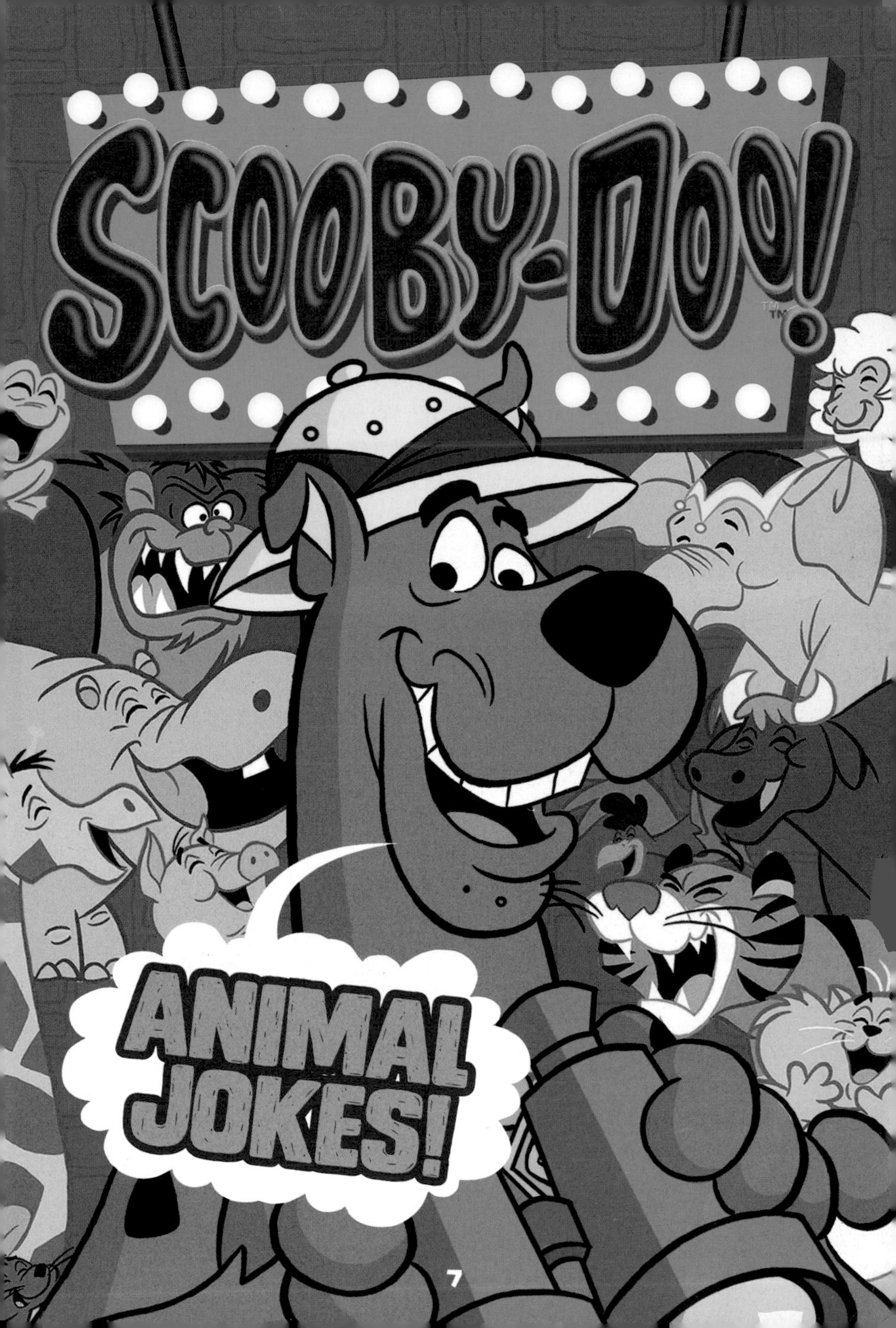
SCOOBY-DOO!™
ANIMAL JOKES!

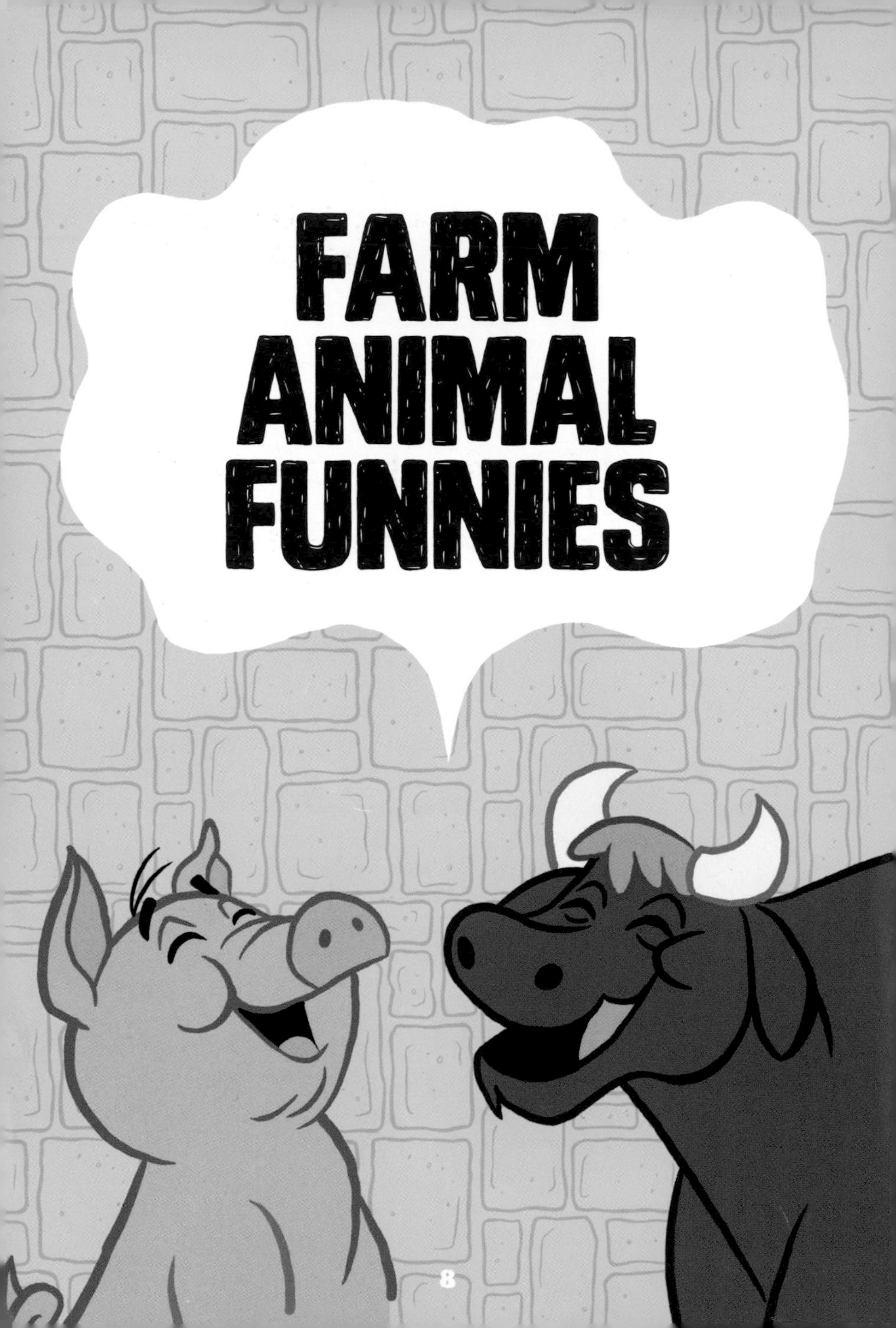
FARM ANIMAL FUNNIES

What time is it when you see six chickens outside?
Easy, it's six a-cluck!

What happened when the cow ran into the barbed wire fence?
Udder **destruction!**

When did the pony answer the teacher's questions?

Whinny had to!

What did the pony say when it fell?
"Help! I can't giddy-up!"

How does a cowboy keep track of his cattle?
He uses a cow-culator!

Why did the sheepdog keep walking along the road?
It didn't see the ewe turn!

Who is a chicken's favorite composer?
Bach! Bach! Bach!

What do you call a really cold cow?
An Eski-moo!

Who's the cow with the sunglasses
and the drumsticks?

He's a moosician.

Where do cows go if they're tired of eating grass?
A calf-ateria!

Where do most horses live?
In a *neigh*-borhood!

What did the chickens do when they lost the baseball game?
They cried fowl!

Why do cows lie down in the rain?

To keep each udder dry.

What do you call the hair on a cow's upper lip?
A moostache.

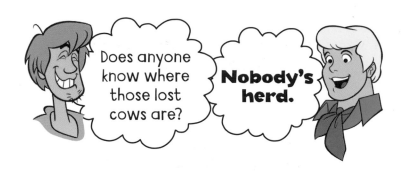

Does anyone know where those lost cows are?

Nobody's herd.

A pig, a cow, and a chicken held up a bank. How did they get caught?

The pig squealed!

What did the chicken say after it laid a square egg?

"Ouch!"

Why did the calf cross the road?
To get to the udder side!

Did you hear about the farmer who thought he was a goat?

He felt that way ever since he was a kid!

How did the sick pig get to the hospital?
In the ham-bulance.

Why do chicken farmers do so well in school?

They're always egg-selling!

If you're a cow, how do you know when it's time to go to sleep?

When it is **pasture bedtime.**

Did you hear about the farmer who needed more room for his pigs?
He built a sty-scraper!

Did you hear about the farmer who drove his cows on a bumpy road?

He wanted a milk shake!

Did you hear about the farmer who crossed a cow with an octopus?

He got an animal that milked itself!

I don't think this cow has any milk.
Well, try the udder one!

Do you know that scientists think they have discovered bones on the moon?

Jinkies! I guess the cow didn't make it!

OUT OF THE BLUE

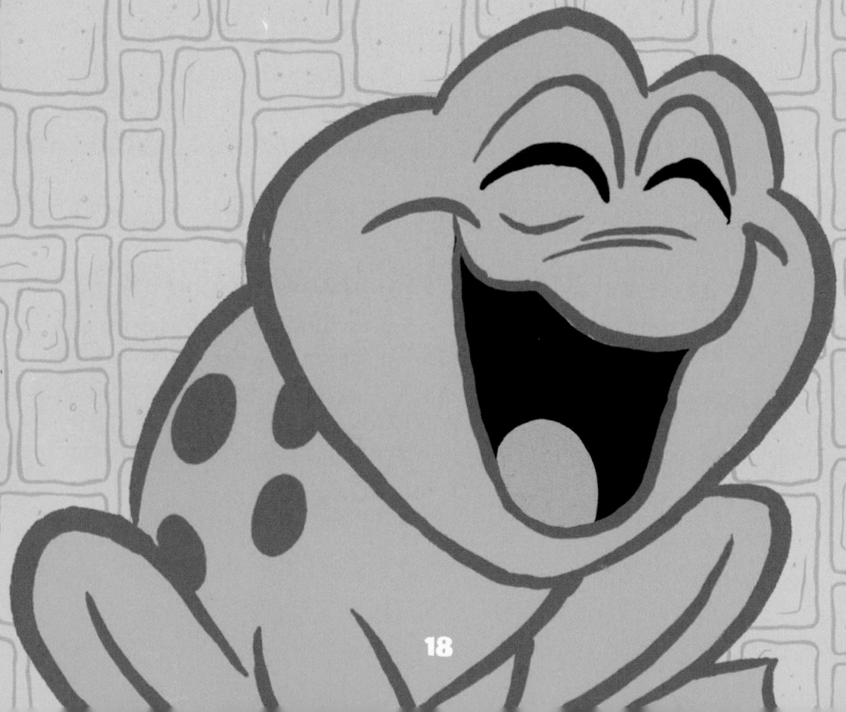

How did the lobster cross the ocean?
It moved from tide to tide.

Did you hear about the guy who thought he was an electric eel?
It was shocking!

Where do dolphins come from?
Finland.

Why do sharks swim in salt water?
Because pepper makes them sneeze!

What do you call photos of a piranha?
Tooth-pics!

When do ducks wake up?
At the *quack* of dawn!

VELMA: Did you know that whales are very musical creatures?

SHAGGY: Really? I suppose that's why they play in orca-stras!

What's the best time to buy canaries?
When they're going "cheep"!

Did you hear about the duck who didn't go "Quack" but went "Moo" instead?
I guess it was learning a "moo" language.

Where does a squid keep its wallet?
In an octopurse.

What did the snail sitting on top of the turtle say?
"Slow doooownn!!!!!"

What do you call a duck that eats gunpowder?
A firequacker!

What do you get if you cross Cinderella with a fish?
Glass flippers!

What do you call a bird that's out of breath?
A puffin.

What kind of bird will steal soap from the bathtub?
A robber duck!

Where does an octopus like to relax?

In an arm-arm-arm-arm-arm-arm-arm-arm chair!

MAN'S BEST FRIEND (AND OTHER PETS)

What dog loves to take bubble baths?
A sham-poodle!

Where do bunnies go if they're sick?
The hop-ital.

What do you call a cheerful bunny?
A hop-timist!

Why did the bunny stop jumping?
It was un-hoppy.

What did you do when you caught Scooby eating the dictionary?

I took the words right out of his mouth!

Did you hear about the mother cat that swallowed a ball of wool?
Yeah, she had mittens!

Where do cat lovers go on vacation?
Purrrr-u!

Why did the rabbit go to the bank?
It needed to *burrow* some money!

Is it easy to buy cat food?

Yes, you can get it *purr* can!

VELMA: What's Shaggy doing out in the yard with a shovel?

FRED: Cleaning up the Scooby-Doo-doo!

FRED: What do you call little dogs that like to visit the library, Scoob?

SCOOBY: Uh, hush puppies?

Why did the rabbit go to the barber?
It was having a bad hare day!

What do you get if you cross a frog and a dog?
A croaker spaniel!

What did Scooby say when he sat on sandpaper?

Ruff!

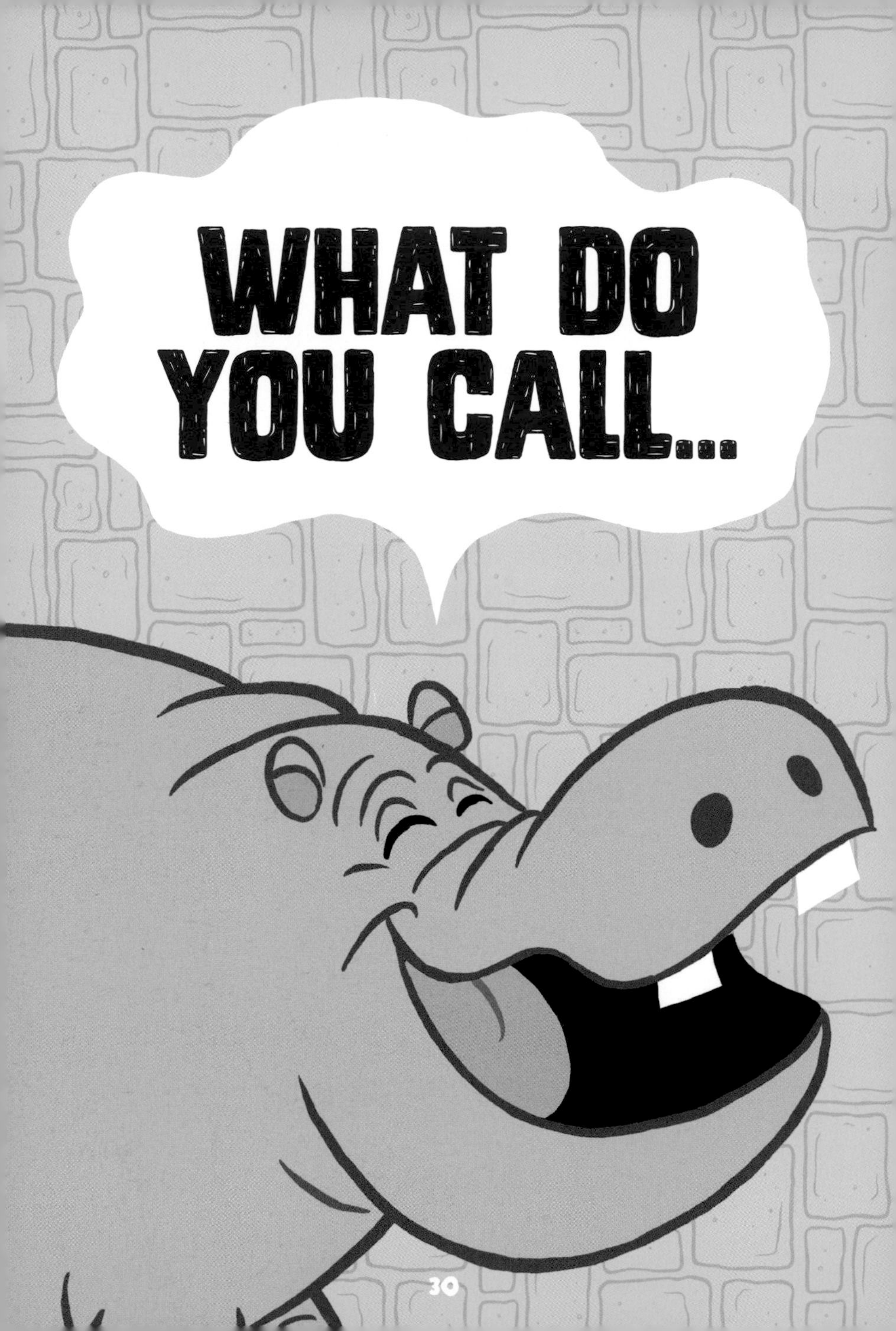
WHAT DO YOU CALL...

... a fish with no eyes?
Fsh.

... a bear with no ears?
B.

... a fly without wings?
A walk.

... a bird on an airplane?
Lazy.

... a lamb with no legs or head?
A sweater!

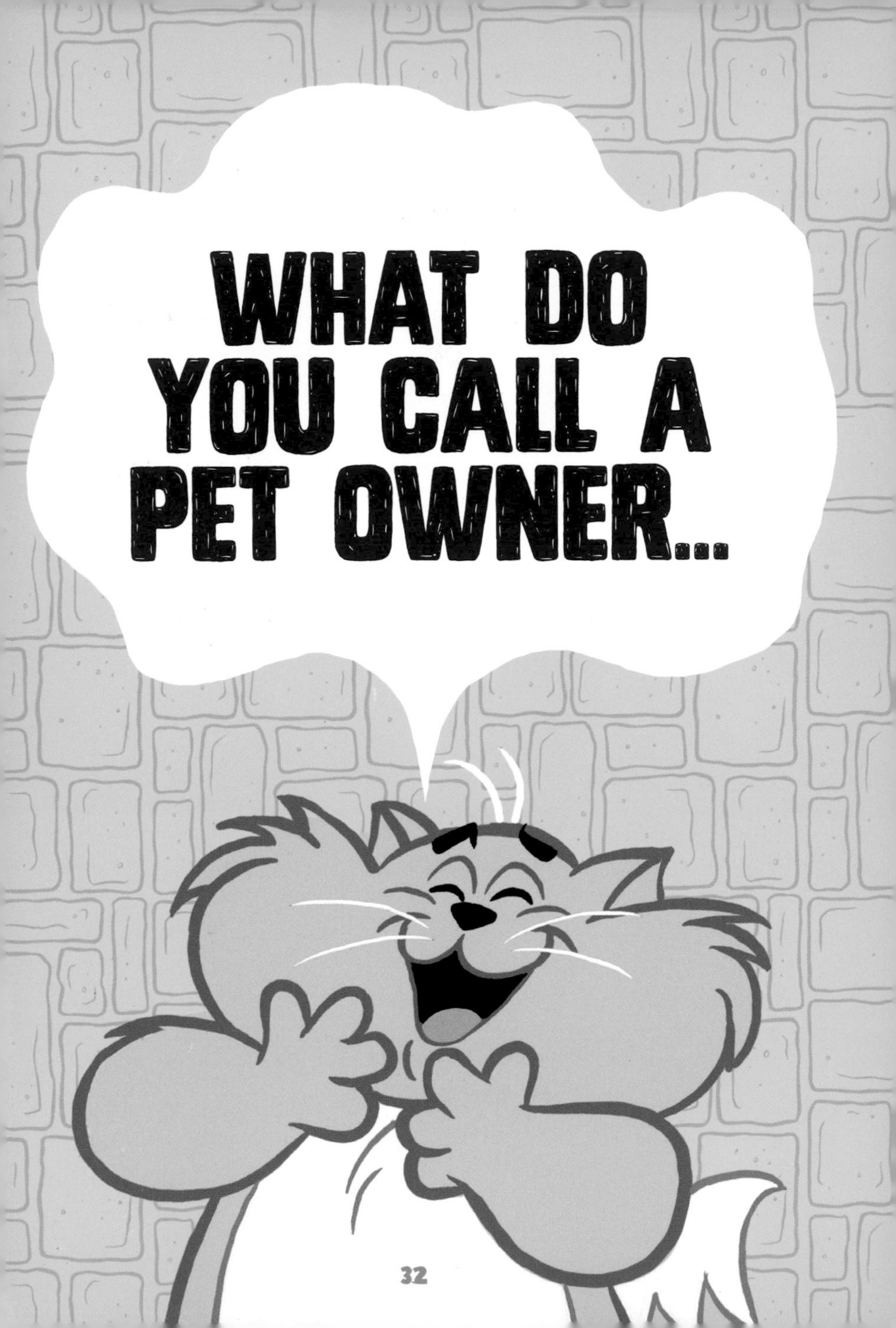
WHAT DO YOU CALL A PET OWNER...

... who has scratches all over his face?
Claude.

... who carries her pet tortoise wherever she goes?
Shelly.

... whose dog always makes holes in the backyard?
Doug.

... who loves to touch all the animals in the
pet store?
Pat.

... who raises bees?
Buzz.

... whose pet camel doesn't have any humps?
Humphrey.

... who put his right hand in a lion's mouth?
Lefty!

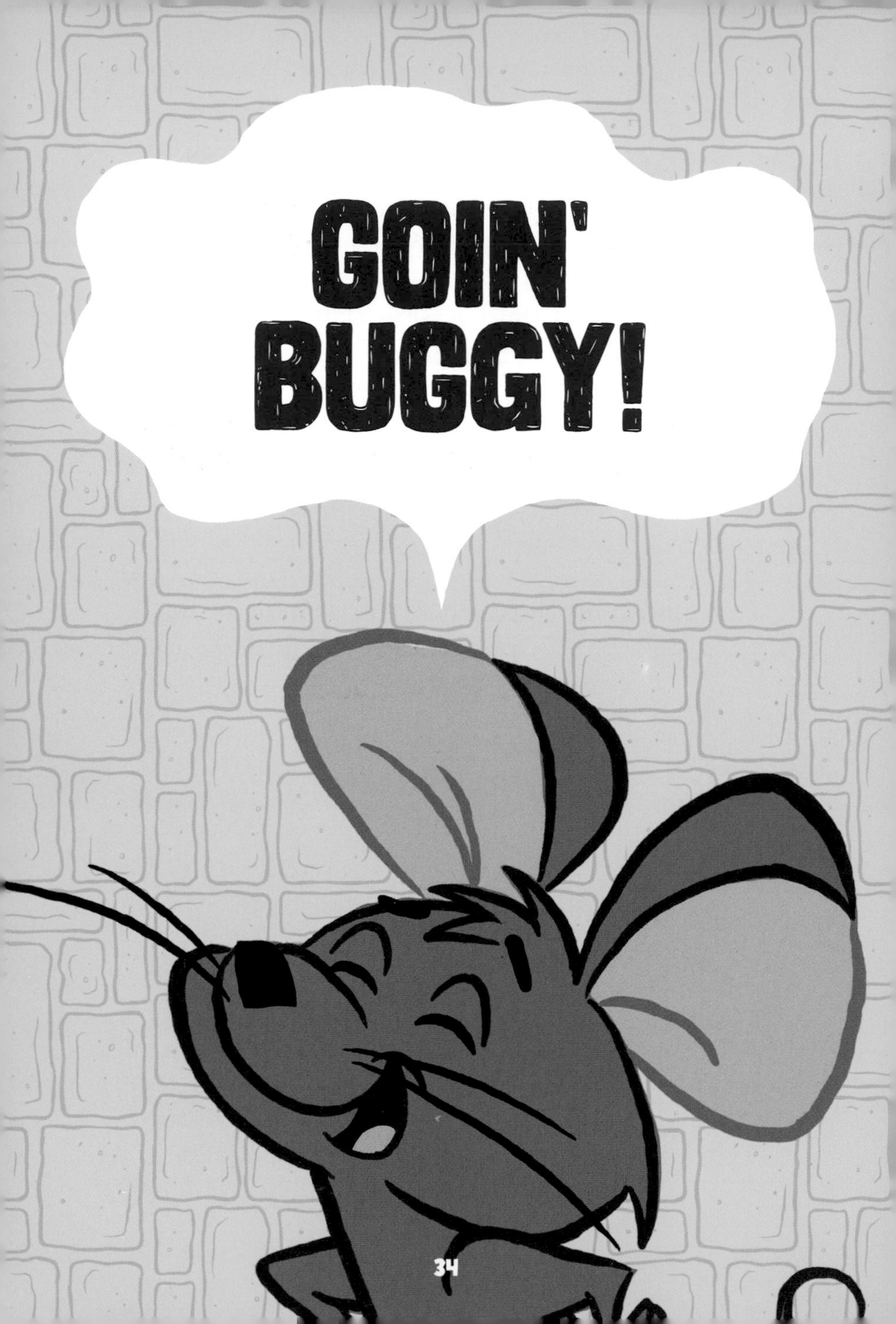
GOIN' BUGGY!

How do you scare away bugs?
Call a SWAT team!

What do termites do when they want to relax?
They take a coffee table break!

How do fleas travel from dog to dog?
They itch-hike!

What does the queen bee do when she burps?
She issues a royal pardon!

What insect flies, drinks blood, and talks in code?
A Morse-quito!

Why was the lightning bug sad?
Because her kids weren't too bright!

What did one flea say to the other?
"Shall we walk or take the dog?"

Name the fastest insect in the world.
The quicket!

How many insects does it take to fill
an apartment?
Ten ants!

What did the termite say when he walked
into the saloon?
"Is the bar tender here?"

How do you find where a flea has bitten you?

Start from scratch!

What do little bees like to chew?
Bumble gum.

What's a mosquito's favorite sport?
Skin-diving!

What has antlers and sucks blood?

A moose-quito!

What are just-married spiders called?
Newly webs!

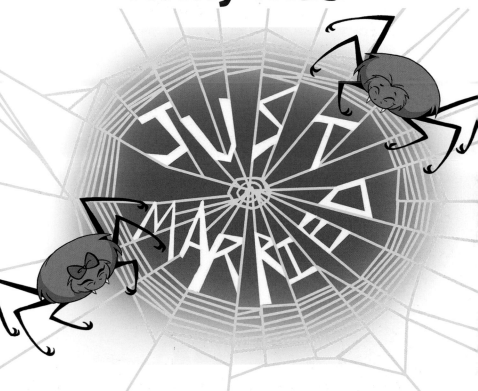

What did the mother worm say to her son when he came home late?
"Where in earth have you been?"

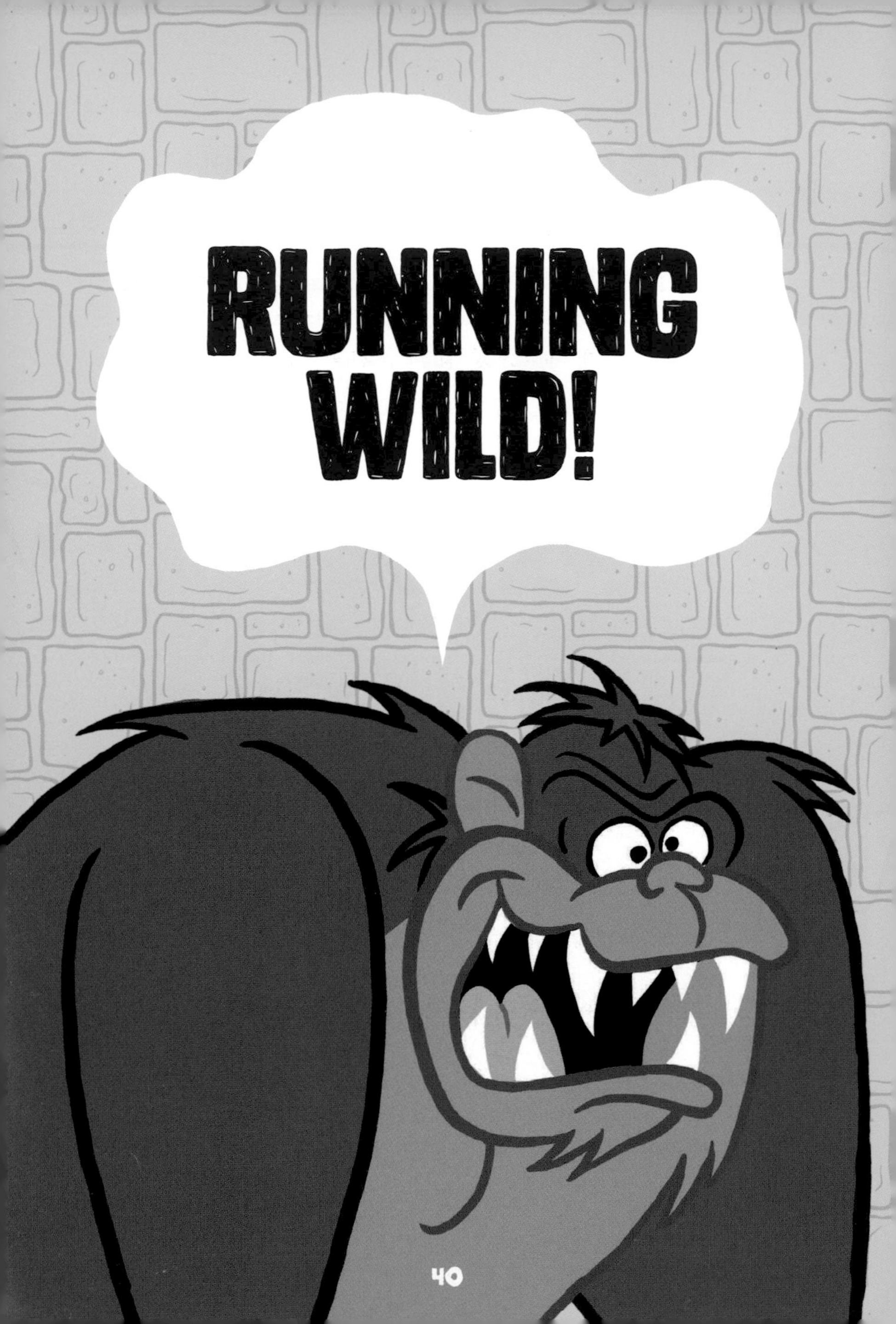
RUNNING WILD!

What happened when Scooby chased the monkey
with a stick of dynamite?
It went BABOOM!

What kind of bear is always wet?
A drizzly bear!

Did you hear the joke about the skunk trapped in the
Mystery Machine?
Never mind. It stinks.

Why was the frog sent home from school?
It was hopper-active!

What did Shaggy say to Fred when they were hiding from the T. rex?
"Doyouthinkhesaurus?"

How do elks send messages to each other?
Moose code.

What's Scooby's favorite snack at the zoo?
Chocolate chimp cookies!

Why do you never see a camel
in the jungle?
Because they're so
good at camel-flage!

What language do polar bears speak?
North Polish.

What happened when the chameleon walked over the feather?
It was tickled pink!

Why did the monkey always wear shoes?
So he didn't have bear feet!

Why did the leopard wear a striped sweater?
So it wouldn't be spotted!

Why did the crocodile cough?
It had a frog in its throat!

What do you call monkeys that are best friends?
Prime-mates!

Why aren't elephants very good dancers?
Because they have two left feet.

I'd like to buy a pair of male deer, please.
That'll be two bucks!

What is big, muddy, has tough skin, and can put people into a trance?
A hypno-potamus!

What is a polar bear's favorite meal?
Ice bergers.

What kind of clothes do kangaroos wear?
Jumpsuits!

What kind of shoes do frogs wear?
Open toad!

What do you call a baby hippo that is still in diapers?
A hippo-potty-mess!

What do you call a lion that eats your mom's sister?
An aunt-eater!

What snakes are the best at math?
Adders.

What is big and gray and gray and gray and gray?

An elephant stuck in a revolving door.

What do you call a gorilla that has bananas growing out of each ear?
**Anything you want.
It can't hear you!**

What is a python's favorite game?
Swallow the leader!

Is it hard to spot a leopard?
No, they come that way.

What kind of music do bunnies like?
Hip-hop!

What does a mother snake do if her baby
snake has a cold?
Viper nose!

Do you know how to make an elephant stew?

Sure. Just keep it waiting for an hour!

How many skunks fit in the Mystery Machine?

Quite a phew!

What did the boa constrictor say to the monkey?
"I've got a *crush* on you!"

Scientists have discovered the bones of a
prehistoric pig.
They're calling it Jurassic Pork!

What do you call a cobra with no clothes on?
Snaked!

What did one toad say to the other?
"Warts new with you?"

What do you call a baby kangaroo that stays indoors?

A *pouch* potato!

What's light and fluffy and swings from trees?
A meringue-utan!

What do you get if you cross an alligator with a bank robber?

A crook-odile!

What did the judge say to the skunk?
"Odor in the court!"

What did the leopard say after dinner?
"That sure hit the spots!"

What did the scale say when the elephant tried to step on it?
"No weigh!"

What kind of animal has white fur, lives at the North Pole, and likes to ride ponies?
A polo bear!

What do you give an elephant that feels sick?

Plenty of room!

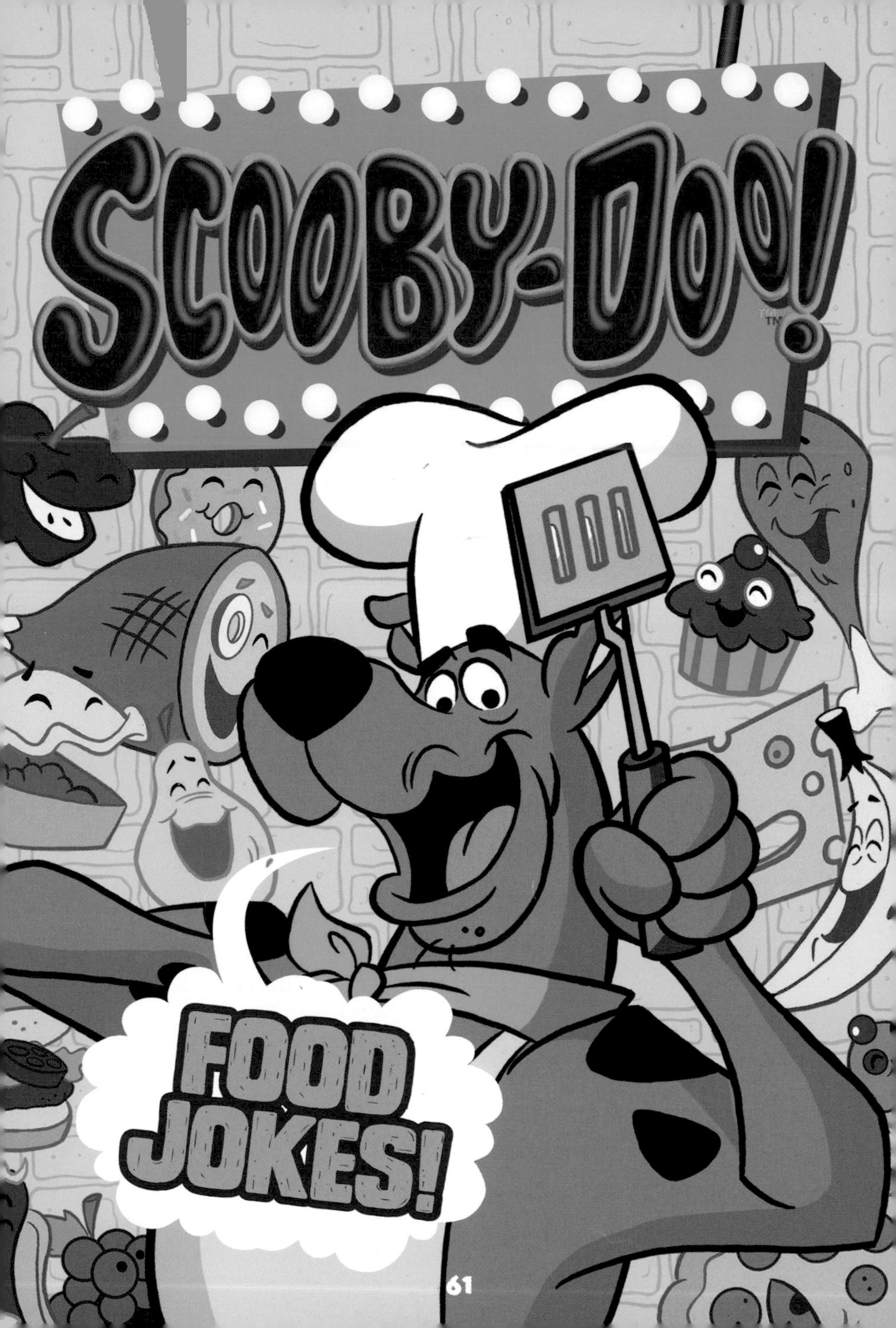
SCOOBY-DOO!
FOOD JOKES!

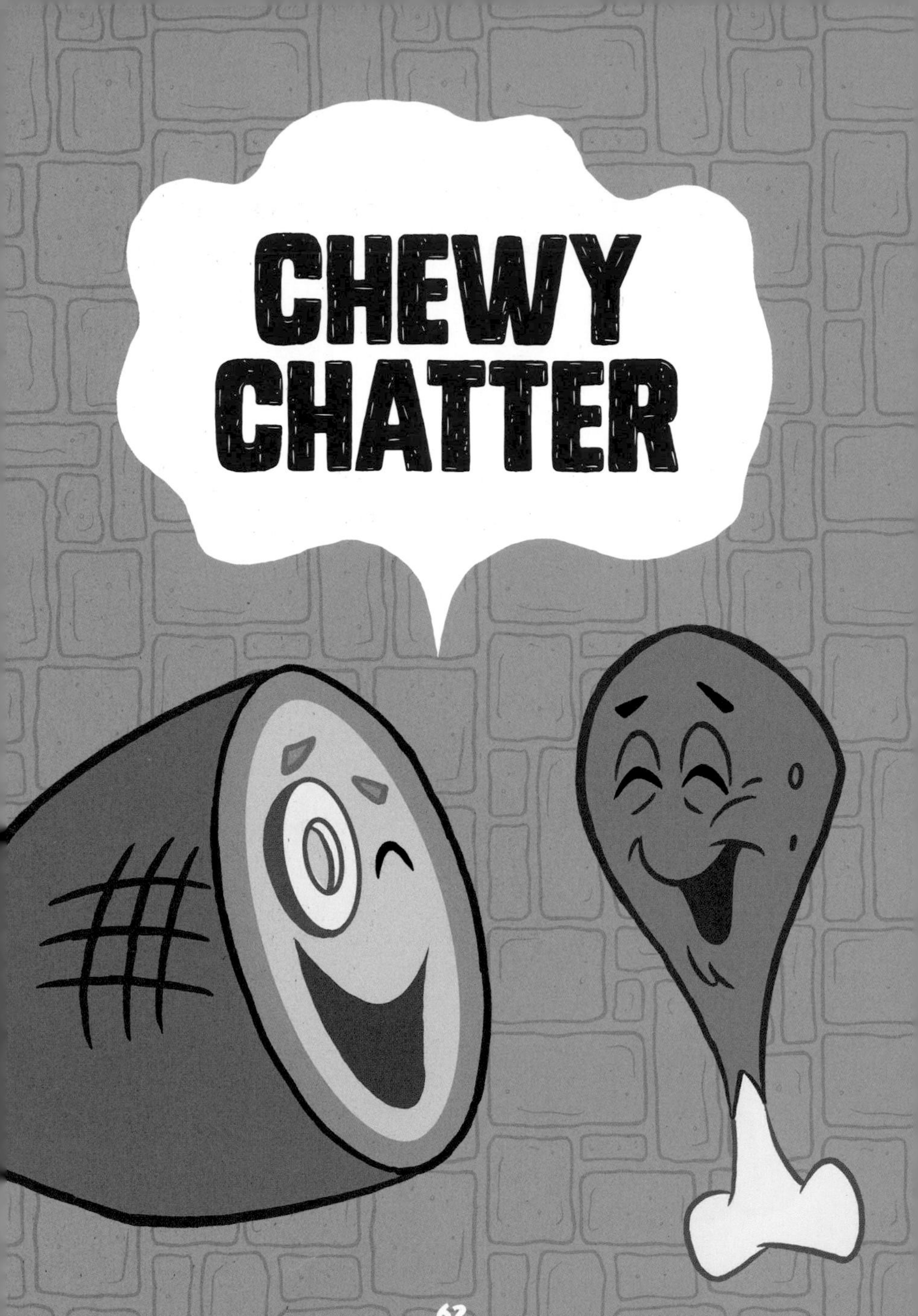
CHEWY CHATTER

What did the nut say when she sneezed?
"Cashew!"

What did the spaghetti say when it got tangled up?
"Knot again!"

What did the tomato say to
the bacon?
**"Lettuce get
together
sometime!"**

What did one steak knife say to the other?
"You look sharp!"

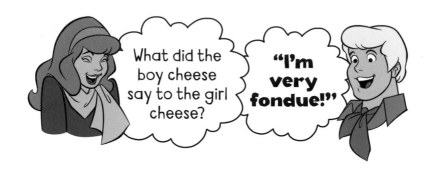

What did one plate say
to the other plate?
"Dinner's on me!"

What did the orange peel say
to the orange?
"I gotcha covered!"

What did the wheel of cheese say when he crossed
the finish line?
"I'm so Gouda at this!"

What did the mother tomato say to the baby tomato
that was following her?

"Come on, ketchup!"

RESTAURANT RIB-TICKLERS

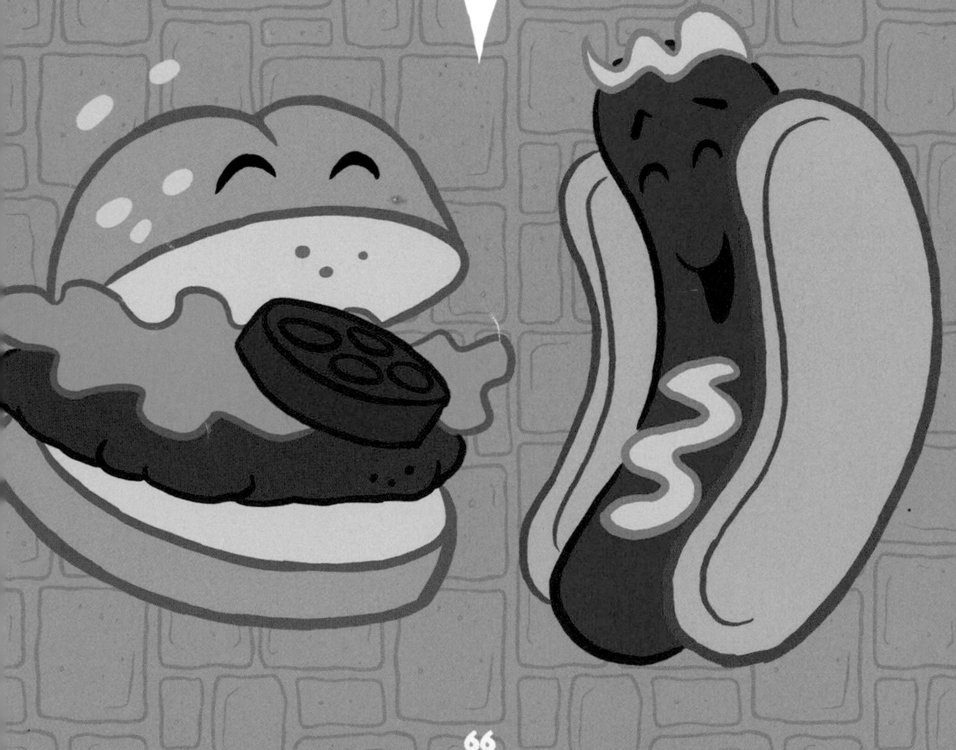

DINER: Excuse me, waiter, but will my pizza be long?
WAITER: No, sir, it will be round.

Did you hear about the neutron that went to the restaurant and ordered a pizza?

"How much do I owe you?" asked the neutron.

The waiter said, **"For you? No charge."**

Why don't you ever see a snail in line at a drive-through?
They don't like *fast* food!

What did the richest man in the world make for dinner every night?
Reservations.

Why was the restaurant chef arrested?

Because he was beating the eggs and whipping the cream!

Why was the customer so angry at the Italian restaurant?

I don't know, but she sure gave the waiter a pizza her mind!

DINER: Sir, why is my food so messy?

WAITER: You told me to *step on it!*

What did the zombie order for lunch?

Pizza, with everyone on it!

NUTRITIOUS KNEE-SLAPPERS

Why did Scooby smear raspberries all over the road?
To go with the traffic jam!

How do you know that carrots are good for your eyes?
Well, have you ever seen a rabbit wearing glasses?

How do you unlock a banana?
With a mon-key!

What does a confused hen lay?
Scrambled eggs!

What kind of nuts do you eat in outer space?
Astronuts.

Why did the orange stop in the middle of the road?
It ran out of juice.

Why did Little Miss Muffet push Humpty Dumpty
off the wall?
He got in her whey.

What happens when a banana gets sunburned?

It peels!

If I had five apples in one hand and six oranges in the other, what would I have?

Really big hands!

How did the pirate pay for the corn?
A buck-an-ear!

Why did the woman divorce the grape?
She was tired of raisin' kids!

Why did the tomato turn red?
It saw the salad dressing!

How do you make an artichoke?
Grab it by the throat!

What's red, round, and has a sore throat?
A hoarse radish!

Why were the raspberries so sad?
Their mom was in a jam!

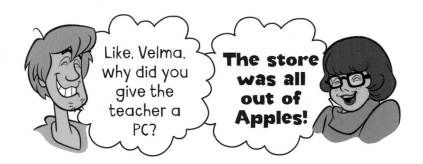

Like, Velma, why did you give the teacher a PC?

The store was all out of Apples!

Shaggy. why are you staring so hard at that carton of orange juice?

Because it says, "Concentrate."

Why did the cabbage win the race?
Because it was *a head!*

What's the difference between a guitar and a fish sandwich?
You can't tuna fish sandwich!

Why were the apples thrown off Noah's Ark?
Only pears were allowed!

Did you hear the joke about the peanut butter?
I better not tell you. You might _spread it!_

What fruit is always teasing the others?
The banana-na-na-na-na!

BELLY LAUGHS FOR BREAKFAST

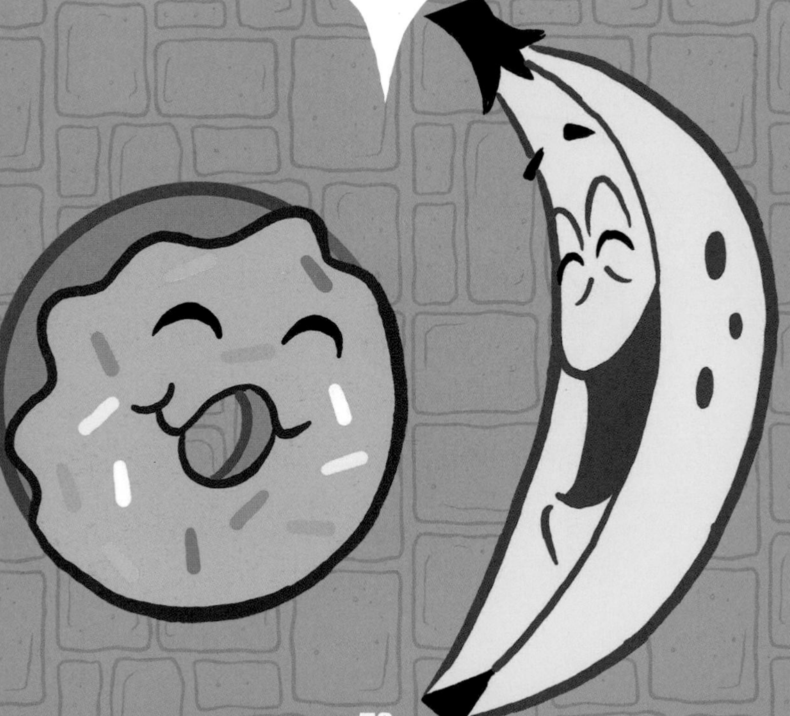

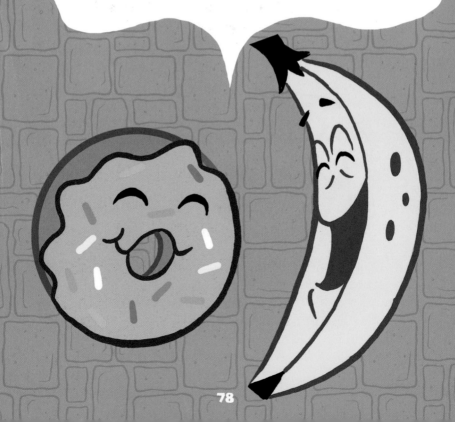

What do mermaids have on toast?
Mermalade.

Where do horses eat their morning cereal?
At the breakfast stable!

How does Darth Vader like his toast?
On the dark side!

What's the best way to get breakfast in bed?
Sleep in the kitchen!

What's red, wiggles, and flies through the air?
A jellycopter.

What did the computer do for breakfast?
It had a byte.

What did the cup say to the tea bag?
"You're in hot water now!"

Why was the cook sad about working in the margarine factory?
She was hoping for something butter!

Why didn't the teddy bear eat his lunch?
He was stuffed!

Why do seagulls fly over the sea?
**If they flew over the bay,
they'd be bagels!**

FAVORITE SCOOBY SNACKS

What do you get when you mix an aardvark
with a pizza?
Ant-chovies!

What do you get when you mix a
porcupine and a cow?
**A steak with built-in
toothpicks!**

What do you get when you mix a golfer with
cocoa, sugar, and whipped cream?
Chocolate putting!

Why do asteroids taste better than ham sandwiches?
Because they're meteor!

What do little dogs eat at the movies?
Pupcorn.

What do you get when you mix a cow, a chicken, and a loaf of bread?

A roost beef sandwich!

What do you get when you mix a centipede with a chicken?

Drumsticks for a month!

LEAST FAVORITE SCOOBY SNACKS

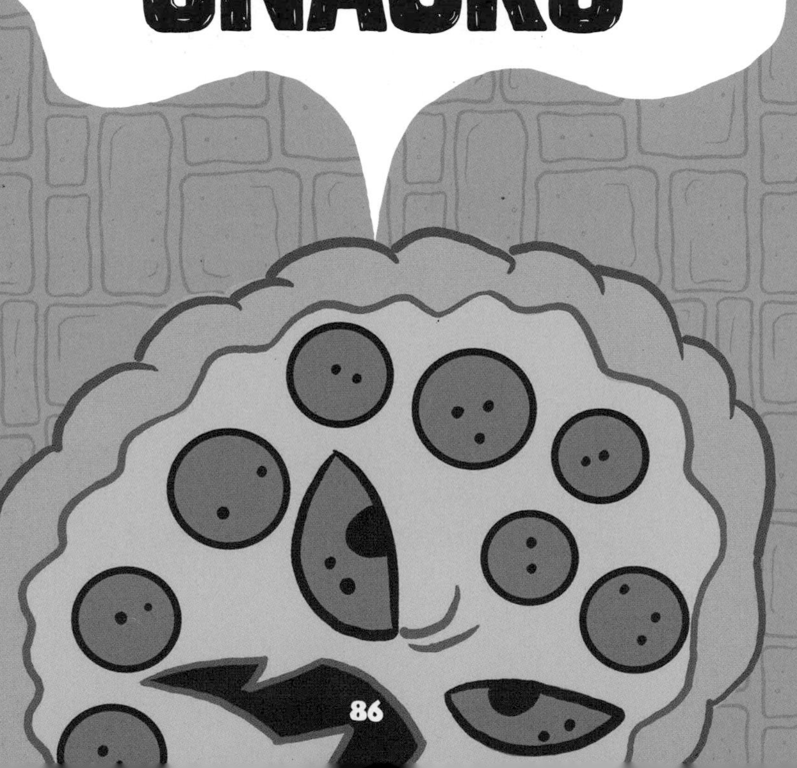

What do you get when you mix a snake with a
bunch of cherries?
A pie-thon!

What did the grape say when the elephant
stepped on it?
Nothing. It just gave a little wine.

What amount of salt can hurt?
A pinch.

Where does Scooby buy his groceries?
At the SUPERmarket!

What do balloons like to drink?
POP!

What does Shaggy serve, but Scooby never eat?
A volleyball.

What do you call a fake noodle?
An impasta!

Why are frogs always so happy?
They eat whatever bugs them!

Why do watermelons have
fancy weddings?
**Because they
can't elope!**

FOOD KNOCK-KNOCKS

Knock, Knock!
Who's there?
Figs.
Figs who?
Figs the doorbell. It's broken!

Knock, Knock!
Who's there?
Olive.
Olive who?
Olive here. Why are you in my house?!

Knock, Knock!
Who's there?
Orange juice.
Orange juice who?
Orange juice coming outside to play?

Knock, Knock!
Who's there?
Dishes.
Dishes who?
Dishes me. Who are you?

Knock, Knock!
Who's there?
Bean.
Bean who?
Bean a while since we talked!

Knock, Knock!
Who's there?
Lettuce.
Lettuce who?
Lettuce in. We're cold!

Knock, Knock!
Who's there?
Doughnut.
Doughnut who?
**Doughnut ask.
It's a secret.**

DELICIOUS DESSERTS

Why did Shaggy eat his math homework?
Because his teacher said it was a piece of cake.

What's white, has a horn, and gives us something good to eat?
The ice cream truck!

Why did the cookie go to the doctor?
He was feeling a little crumby.

How do you make a milk shake?
Take it to a scary movie!

Why did the baker stop making doughnuts?
She was tired of the hole business.

What does chocolate do when it hears a good joke?
It snickers.

What kind of dessert roams the Arctic tundra?
Moose!

Why did Scooby go to the doctor after
eating the cupcakes?
Because he got frostingbite.

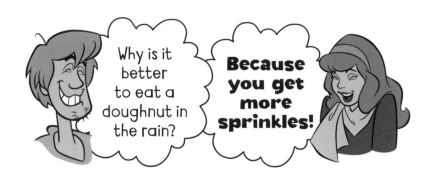

KID: How much for a taste of
the gingerbread?
**WITCH: Don't worry.
It's on the house!**

How does the Mystery gang make cookies?
With Scooby-dough!

Why don't they serve chocolate in prisons?
Because if the prisoners eat too much, some of them might break out!

What's big and white and lives on Mars?

A Martian-mallow?

DINER: Do you have ice cream on the menu today?
WAITER: No, I wiped it off.

Who can serve ice cream faster than a speeding bullet?
Scooperman!

What's a math teacher's favorite dessert?
Pi.

What grows high in a tree and likes to eat chocolate?
A cocoa-nut.

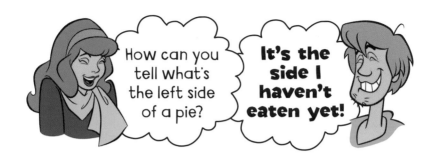

Why did the student work at the bakery?

Because she *kneaded* the dough!

MORE FOOD FUNNIES

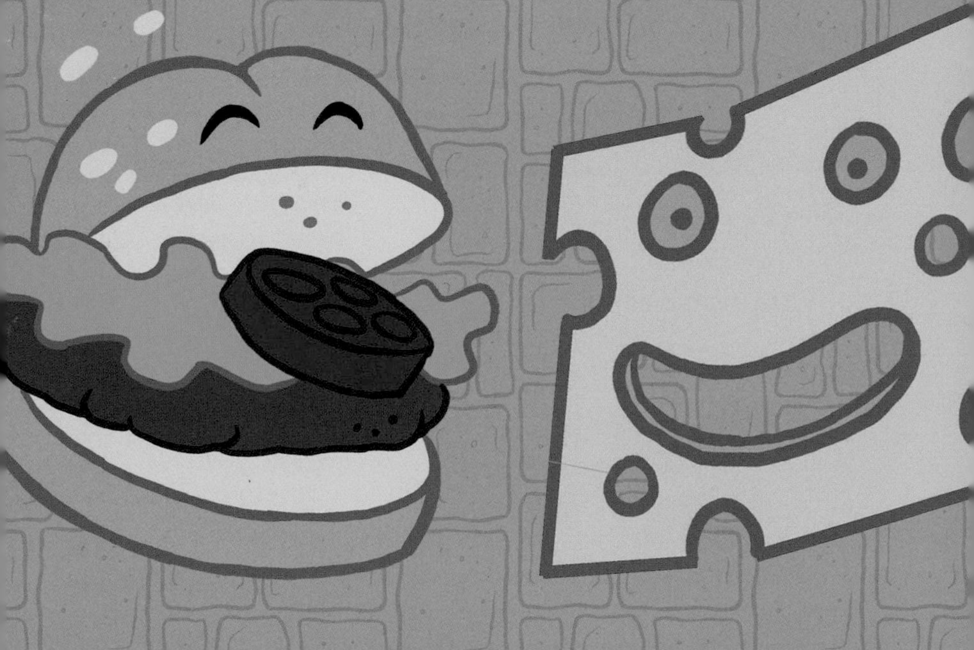

What do you call cheese that is sad?
Blue cheese!

What did the TV dinner say after it was packaged?
"Curses! Foiled again!"

What happened to the caveman who saw a sheep
struck by lightning?
He invented the baa-becue!

Why can't you ever starve on a beach?
**Because of all the
sand which is there!**

Why did the doctor give mustard to Scooby
when he had a fever?
**Mustard is the best thing for
a hot dog!**

What do you call a pig that just got over a cold?
A cured ham!

What does a pirate like on his salad?
Thousand Island dressing!

How can you tell if a clock is hungry?
It always goes back four seconds.

Why is six afraid of seven?
Because seven eight nine!

Why couldn't the sesame seed stop gambling?
Because she was on a roll!

SCOOBY:
When do we get to eat?

**ASTRONAUT:
At launch time!**

Where were the first chickens fried?
In Greece!

What's the world's heaviest soup?
Won-ton soup!

What kind of cup is impossible to drink out of?
A hiccup!

I hear polar bears like Mexican food.
Yeah, especially brrr-itos!

What did the police do with the hamburger?
They grilled it!

What do whales eat for lunch?
Peanut blubber sandwiches!

What did the soda say to the bottle opener?
"Can you help me find my pop?"

What's the best day of the week to eat chicken?

Fryday!

What snack do you get when a chicken sits on the roof?
Egg rolls!

What cheese is made backwards?
Edam.

Why did the light bulb get bigger and bigger?
He kept eating watts and watts!

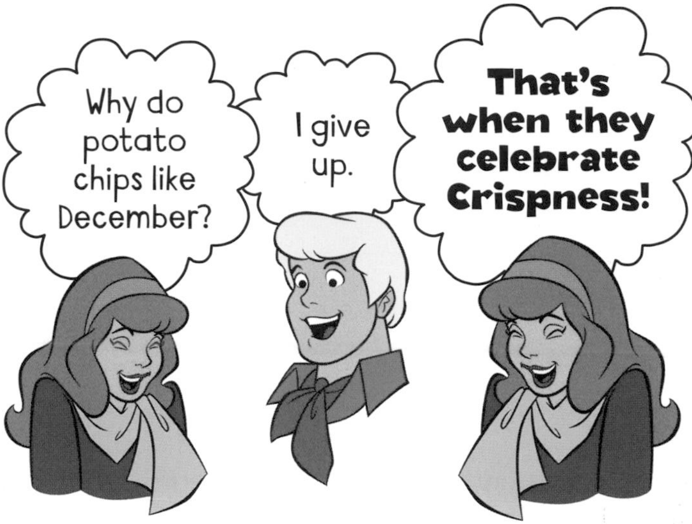
Why do potato chips like December?
I give up.
That's when they celebrate Crispness!

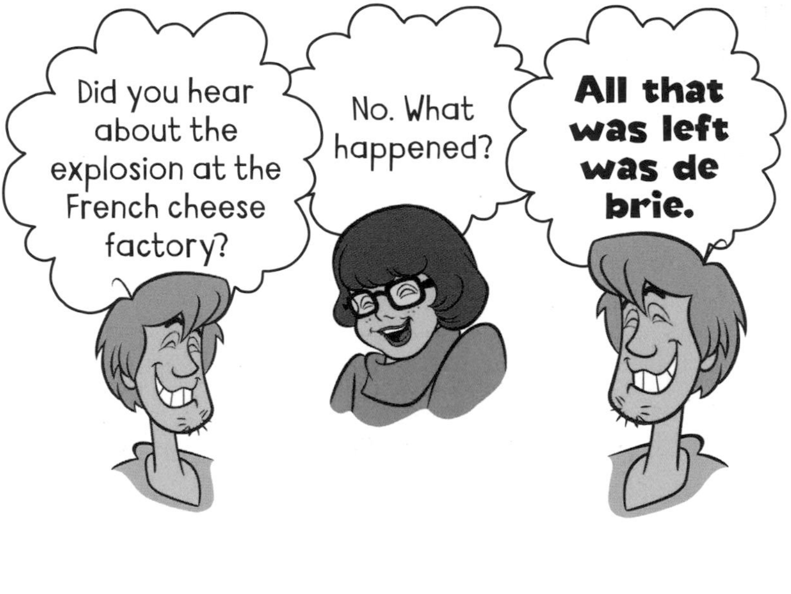
Did you hear about the explosion at the French cheese factory?
No. What happened?
All that was left was de brie.

What did the hamburger name her daughter?
Patty.

What do you call cheese that isn't yours?
Nacho cheese!

What do you get if you cross a duck with a cow?
Milk and quackers!

Where did the spaghetti go to dance?
The meat ball!

Scoob, why isn't your
salad joke in this book?

**It was
tossed!**

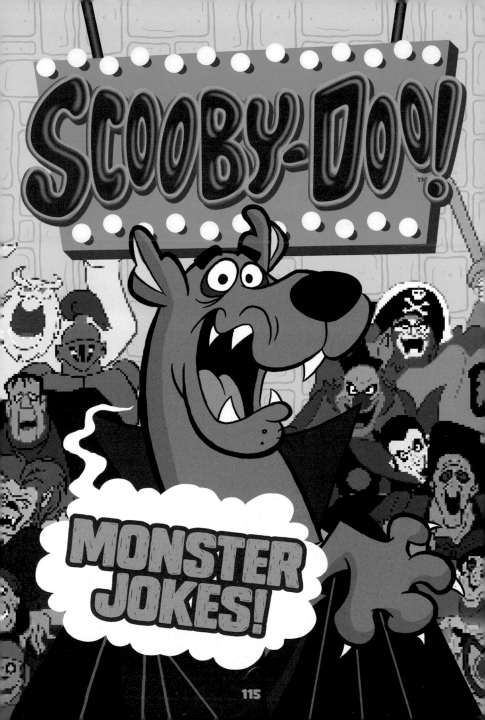

SCOOBY-DOO!

MONSTER JOKES!

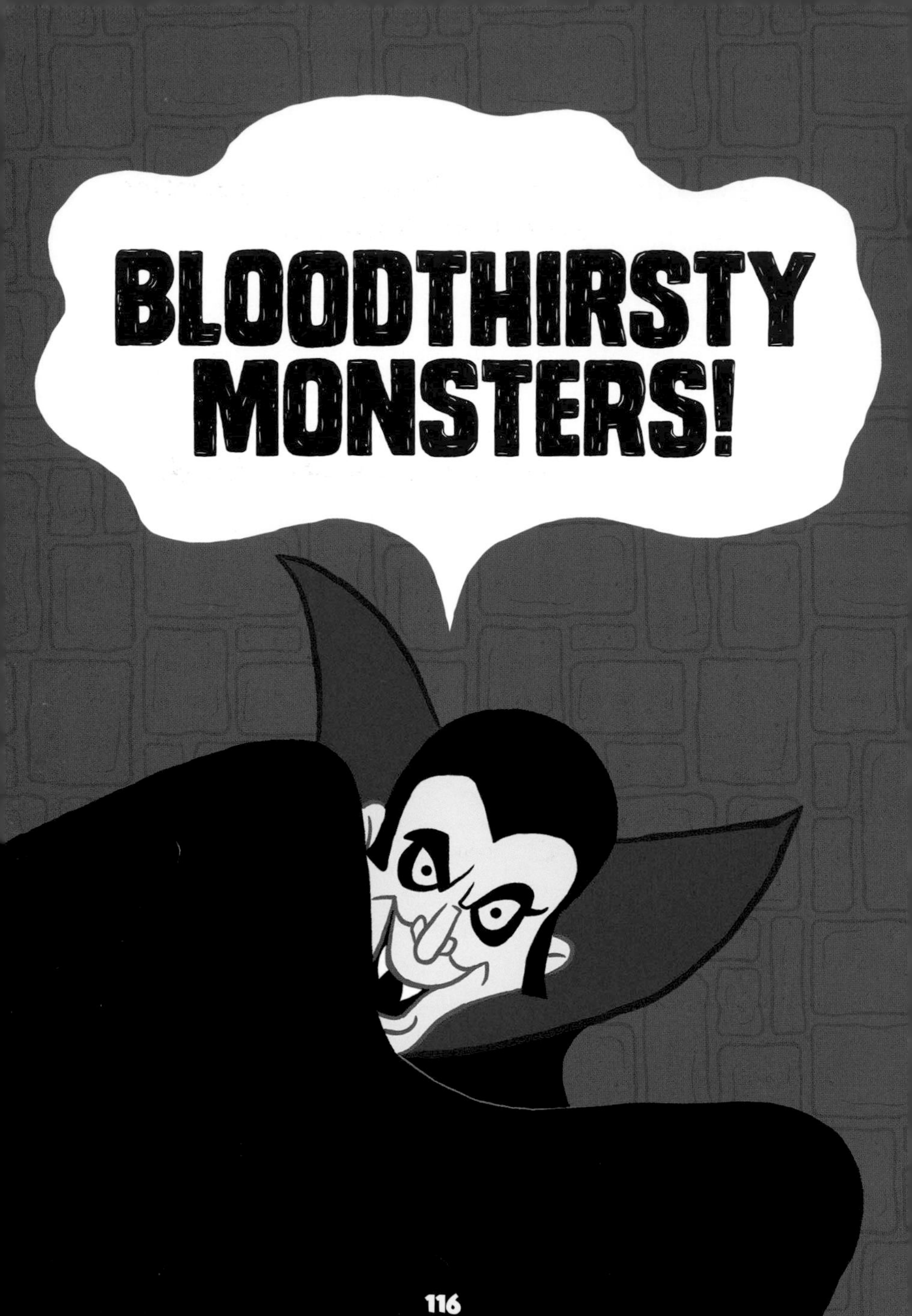
BLOODTHIRSTY MONSTERS!

What's the best way to help a starving zombie?
Give him a hand!

When do zombies go to sleep?
Only when they're dead tired.

What do zombies like eating the most in a restaurant?

The waiters!

Where's the safest place in your house to hide from zombies?
The *living* room, of course.

What does Godzilla call skateboarders?

Meals on wheels!

Why is Godzilla so good at sneaking up on people?
He's a crept-tile.

What did Godzilla say when he saw a rush-hour train full of passengers?
"Chew-chew!"

What's the best way to speak to Godzilla?
Long distance!

Why did Godzilla eat all the furniture in the hotel room?
He had a suite tooth!

Did you hear that Godzilla got sick and threw up?
Yeah, it's all over town!

What do you call Godzilla in a phone booth?

Stuck!

How does Dracula like his coffee?
De-coffin-ated!

When did Dracula realize that sunlight could destroy him?

When it finally *dawned* on him!

What kind of dog does Dracula have?
A bloodhound!

Why won't anyone kiss Dracula?
He has *bat* breath!

Why was the vampire studying all night long?
She was getting ready for her blood test!

What do you say to a vampire who wants to go on a date?
"Fangs, but no fangs!"

Why don't vampires have many friends?

They're such pains in the neck!

What's a vampire's favorite fruit?
Neck-tarines.

Why did the zombie lose the card game?
He had a rotten hand!

What do you call a zombie
door-to-door salesman?

A dead-ringer!

What happened when the zombie was late for the dinner party?

They gave him the cold shoulder.

What do you call a teenage zombie with no legs?

Grounded.

What did the zombie do when she lost her hand?

She went to the *secondhand* store!

What did the little zombie make of his new friends at school?

A pie!

What did the zombie eat after the dentist pulled out all his teeth?

The dentist!

Don't make a vampire angry. **They have very *bat* tempers!**

What does Dracula take when he has a cold?
Coffin medicine!

What do goblins like to put on their bagels?
Scream cheese!

That vampire sure is popular.

Yeah, she has a big fang club.

How did the vampire cure his sore throat?
He spent all day gargoyling!

What do little vampires eat for lunch?
Alpha-bat soup.

Where does Dracula keep his money?
In a blood bank.

Why don't vampires ever race each other?
They're always neck and neck!

Did you know there's a vampire duck?
Of course. It's Count Quackula!

Why did the vampire flunk out of art class?
She could only *draw blood!*

I heard the new restaurant has a vampire for a chef.
Yes, he's Count Spatula!

What do you get if you cross the Mystery Machine with a bloodsucker?

A van-pire!

PHANTOMS, SPIRITS, AND SPOOKS!

What do you call a ghost's mom and dad?
Trans-parents!

What do you call a haunted chicken?
A poultry-geist!

What keeps a ghost cool in the summer?
The scare conditioner.

What did the ghost wear to the fancy dinner?
A boo tie!

In what position do ghosts sleep?
Horror-zontal!

Where do ghosts go for treats?
The I-scream parlor!

What's a phantom's favorite game?
Hide-and-ghost-seek!

What do you say to a ghost when you meet one?
"How do you boo?"

What do baby ghosts wear on their feet?
Boo-ties!

Did you hear that
Dr. Frankenstein combined a
cocker spaniel, a poodle,
and a ghost?

Yup, he ended up with a cocker-poodle-boo!

When do ghosts wake up?

In the moaning!

What do teenage ghosts wear?
Boo jeans.

What's the first thing ghosts do when they get in a car?
Put on their sheet belts!

Why are ghosts so bad at telling lies?
You can always see right through them.

How do ghosts like their eggs for breakfast?
Terror-fried!

Why do ghosts like riding in elevators?
It raises their spirits!

Did you know that ghost has a girlfriend?

Yes, but I don't know what she sees in him!

MAD SCIENTIST JOKES!

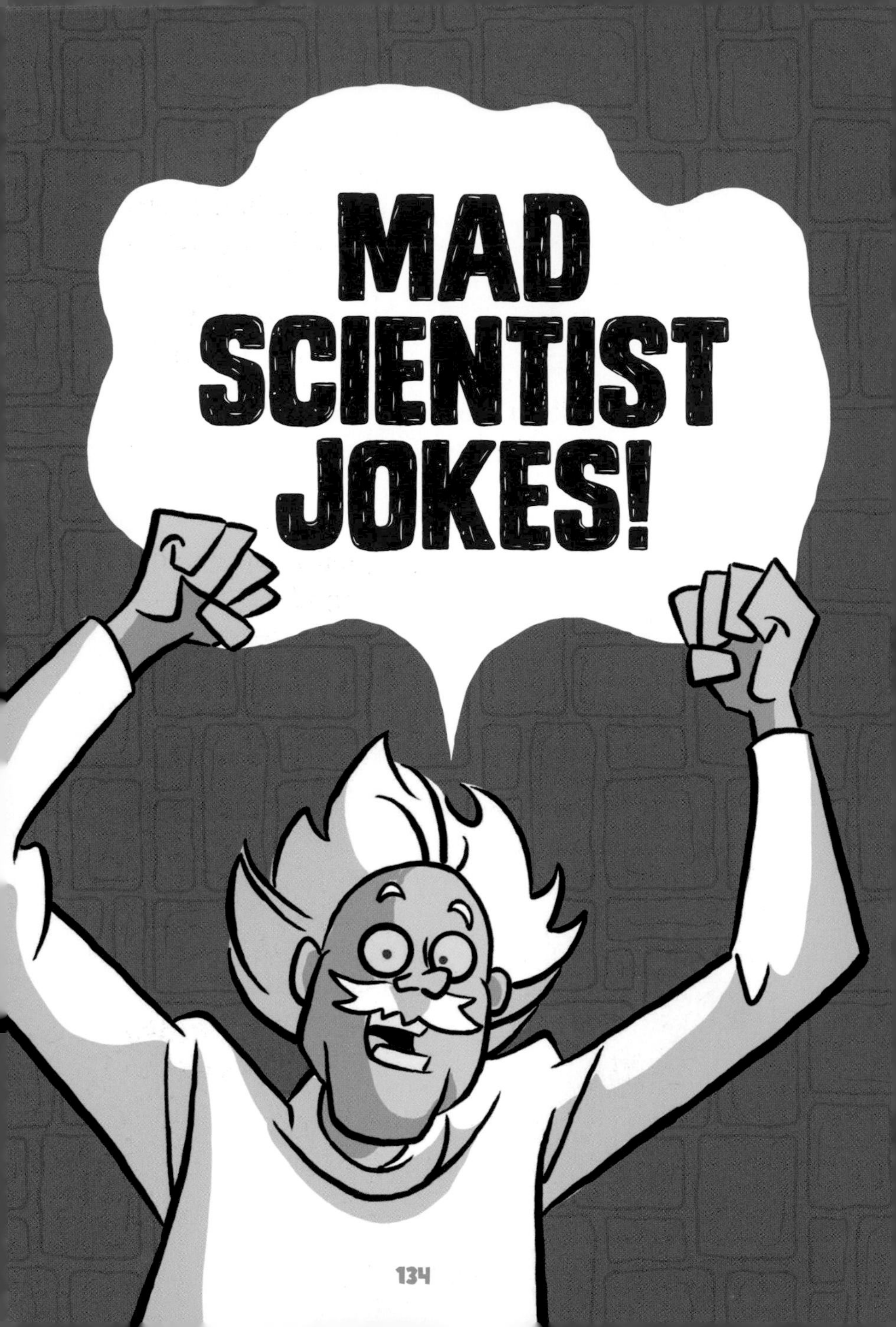

What happened to
the mad scientist who
crossed a pig with a
grizzly?

**He got a
teddy boar!**

What happened to
the mad scientist who
crossed a UFO with a
wizard?

**He got a
flying sorcerer!**

What happened to
the mad scientist who
crossed a slab of cheese
with Frankenstein?

**He got a really
scary Muenster!**

What happened to the
mad scientist who crossed
a snake with a Lego set?
**He got a
boa constructor!**

What happened to
the mad scientist who
crossed a turtle with a
porcupine?
**He got a
slowpoke.**

What happened to
the mad scientist who
crossed a toad with a
distant galaxy?
**He got star
warts!**

What happened to the mad scientist who crossed a bear cub with a skunk?

He got Winnie the Phew!

What happened to the mad scientist who crossed a newborn snake with a trampoline?

He got a bouncing baby boa!

What happened to the mad scientist who crossed an alligator with a bunny?

He had to get a new bunny!

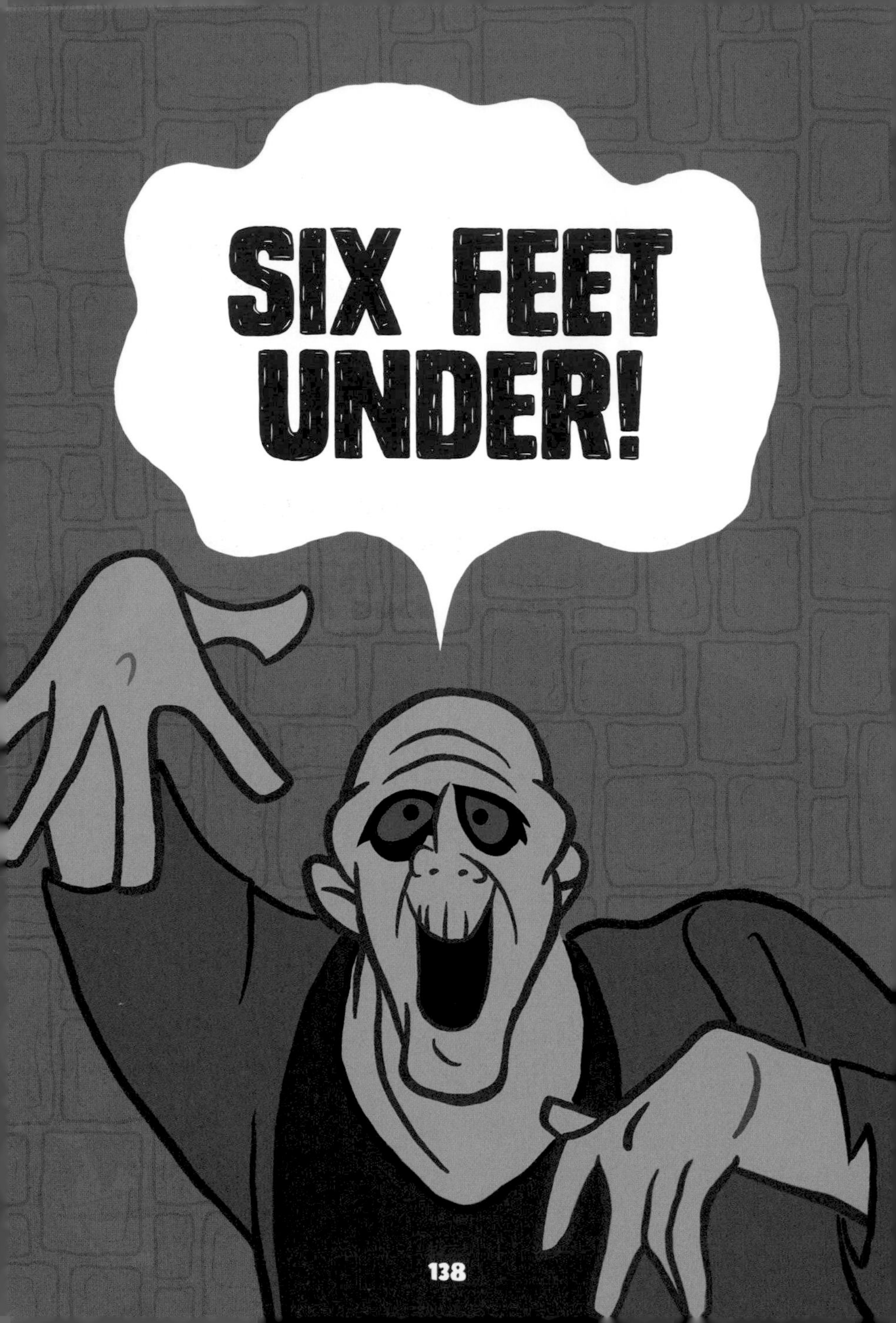
SIX FEET UNDER!

Why didn't the skeleton go to the school dance?
He had no *body* to go with!

Why was the skeleton so afraid of heights?
She just didn't have the guts!

Why did the skeleton keep his head in the freezer?
I guess he was a numbskull!

Why didn't the skeleton eat the cafeteria food?
He didn't have the stomach for it.

Where do skeletons go for vacation?
The Dead Sea!

Where can you always find a cemetery?
In the dead center of town.

What did the movie director say when she had
finished her mummy movie?
"That's a wrap!"

The doctor told the mummy he has the heart of a
much younger man.
**Yes, and the doctor told him he had
to give it back, too!**

Did you know that skeletons love riding motorcycles?
Yup, they're *bone* to be wild!

What do skeletons order at restaurants?
Spare ribs!

What did the father skeleton say to his son who stayed in bed all day?

"Lazy bones!"

Why doesn't the mummy have any friends?
She's too *wrapped up* in herself!

What did the ghoul say to his ghoulfriend?
"I really dig you!"

What does a skeleton say before every meal?
"Bone appétit!"

Who won the skeleton beauty contest?
No body!

Cemeteries are having a hard time finding room for all their guests.

Yes, it's a *grave* problem!

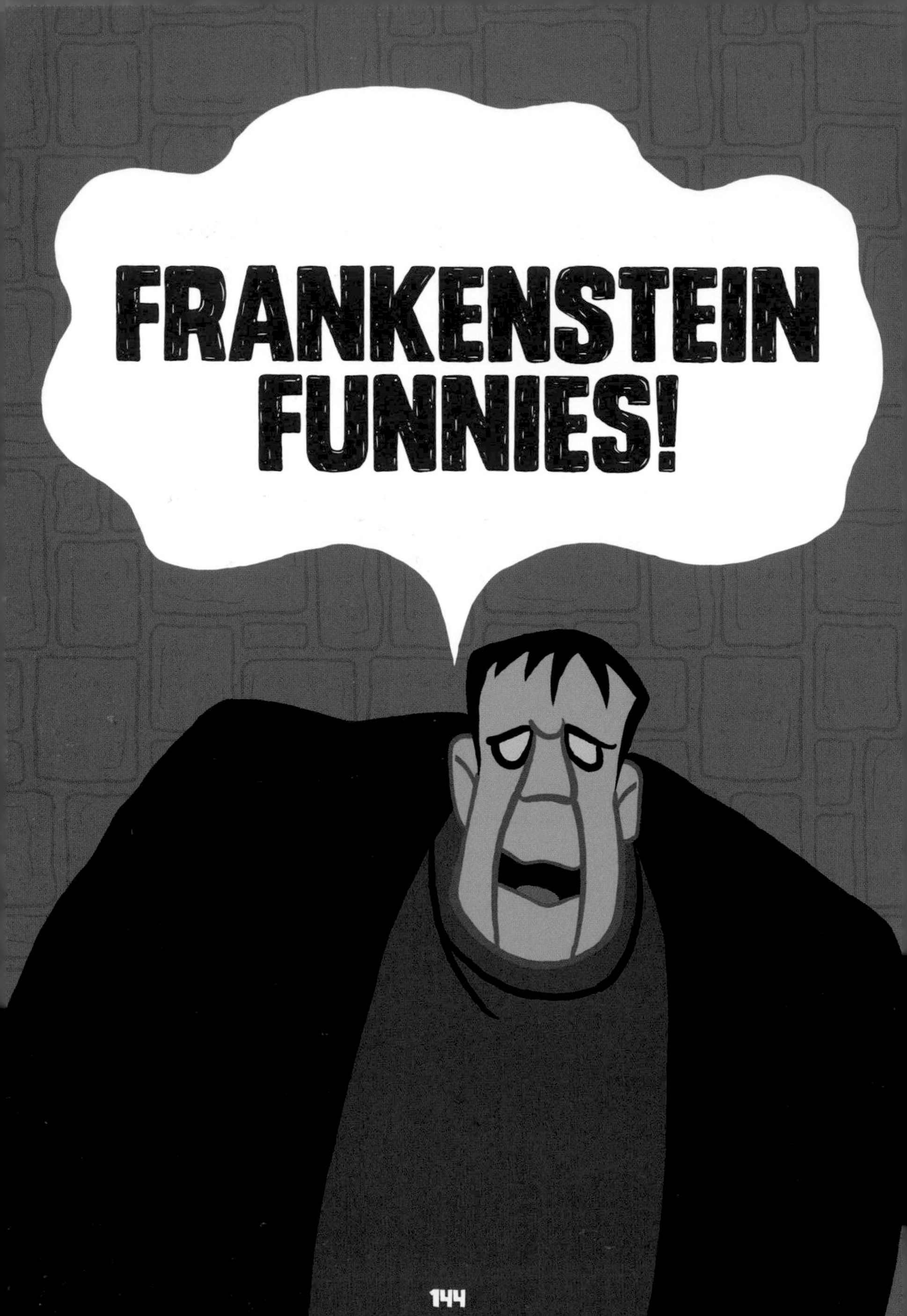
FRANKENSTEIN FUNNIES!

Why did Frankenstein go to the psychiatrist?
He thought he had a screw loose!

Why did Frankenstein go to the restaurant
with a raisin?
He couldn't find a date!

What's Frankenstein's favorite dessert?
I scream!!!

Do you know where Frankenstein lives?
Sure, he's on a dead end.

I heard Dr. Frankenstein is a funny guy.
Yeah, he always keeps you in *stitches*!

Why is Dr. Frankenstein so popular?

He's very good at making friends.

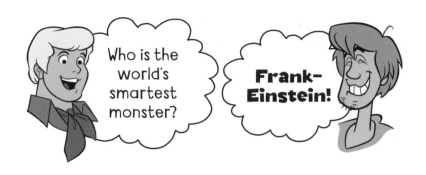

Who is the world's smartest monster?

Frank-Einstein!

What did one of Frankenstein's ears say to the other?
"I didn't know we lived on the same block!"

What does it say on Frankenstein's gravestone?
"Rest in Pieces."

How did Frankenstein get rid of his headache?
He put his head through the window and the pane just disappeared!

What did Frankenstein say to the screwdriver?
"Daddy!"

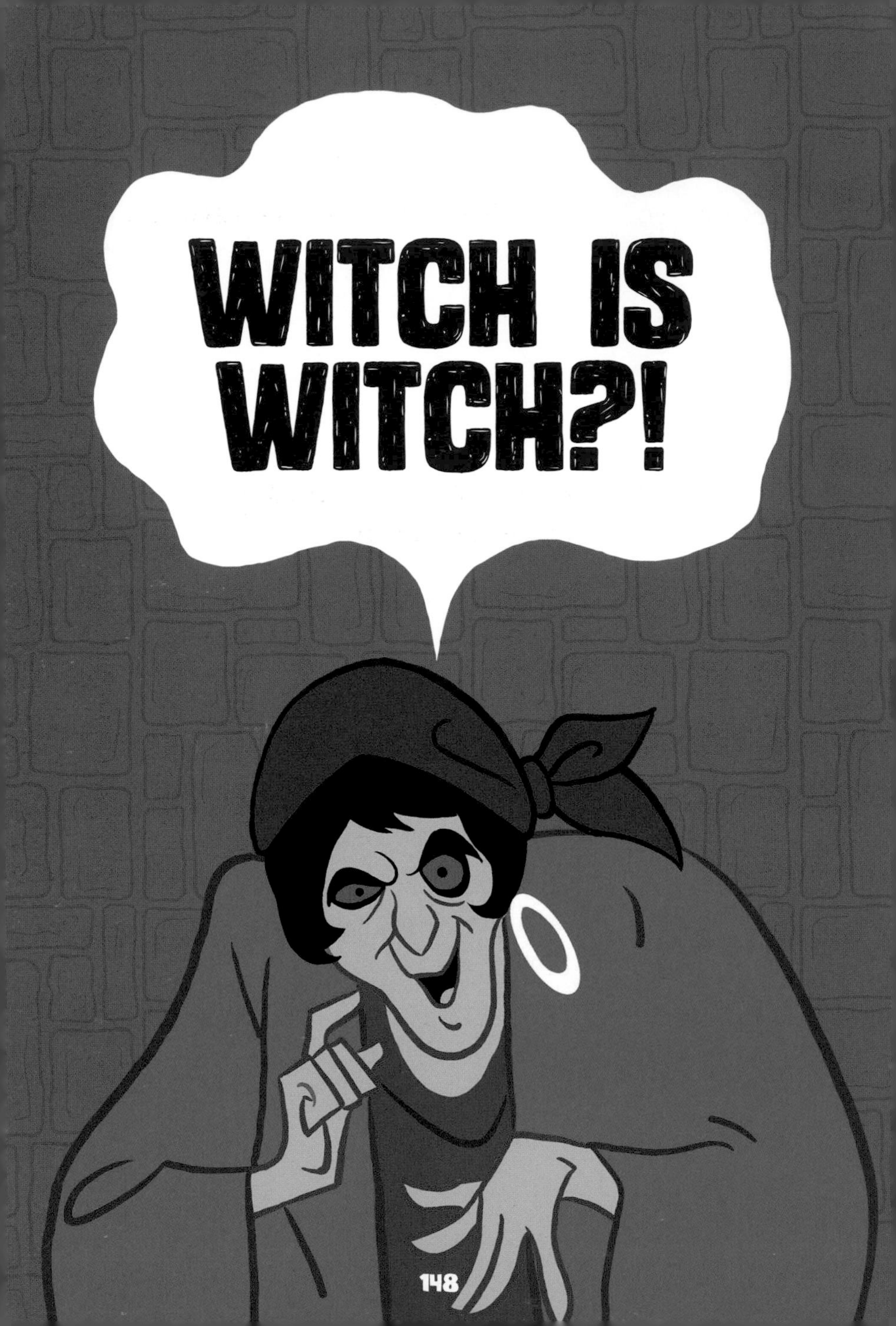
WITCH IS WITCH?!

What do you call witches who live in the same room?
Broom-mates!

What do you call a nervous witch?
A twitch!

Watch out! We're being chased by twin sorceresses!
I know! I can't tell witch is witch!

Why was the witch late for the party?
Her broom overswept.

What did the sorceress have for a snack?

A sand-witch!

How does a wizard tell time?
With a witch-watch!

What do you get when you cross a witch's cat with a lemon?
A sourpuss.

Did you know that witches fall from the sky?
Yeah, and the angry ones fly off the handle!

What happened to the sorcerer who was thrown out of school?

He was ex-*spelled!*

What kind of sorceress is always helpful in the dark?

A lights-witch!

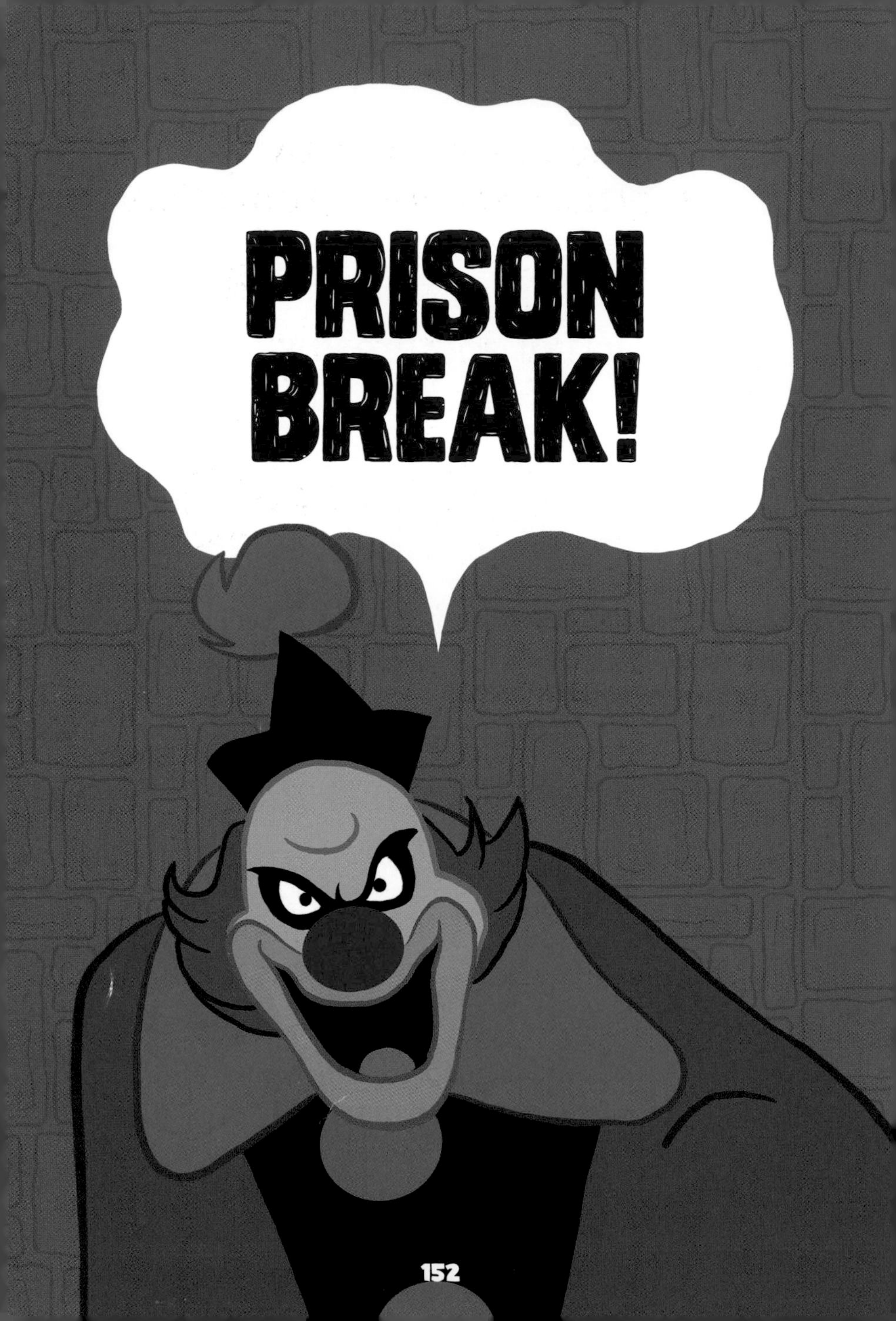
PRISON BREAK!

What happened when the giant brick monster escaped from prison?

They set up a road block!

What happened when the Human Fly
escaped from prison?
They brought in a SWAT team!

What happened when the Cyclops escaped
from prison?
The police had to keep an eye open!

What happened when the evil
hairstylist escaped from prison?

Police had to comb the area!

What happened when the mutant corn monster escaped from prison?

They called out the cobs!

What happened when a gang of monsters escaped through the sewers?

The police said it was a grime wave!

WEREWOLVES, ALIENS, AND OTHER CREEPY CRAWLIES!

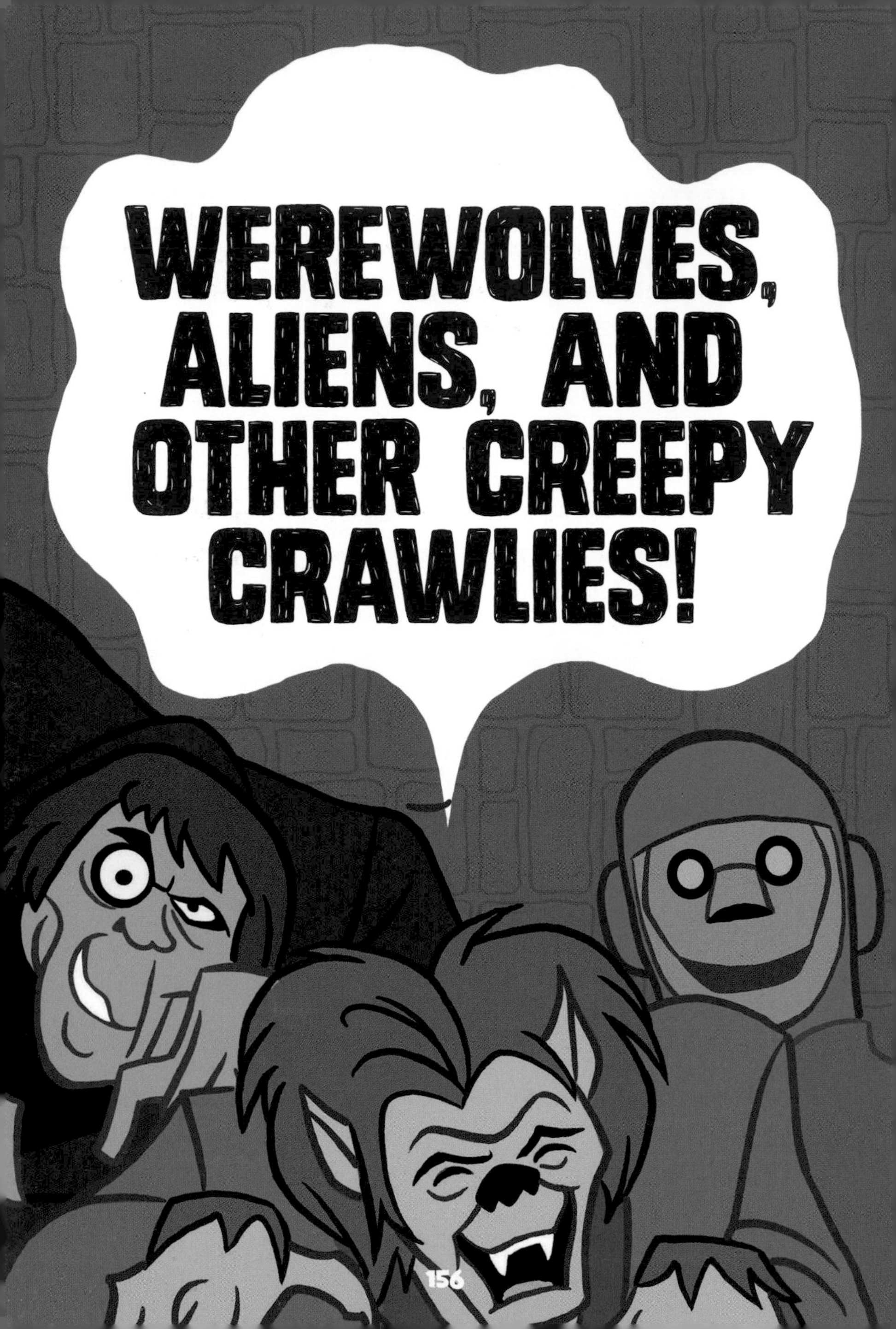

Why didn't the monster ever go out with his friends after school?
He wasn't allowed to play with his food!

How many parents does a werewolf have?
Five. One ma and four paws.

What does a techno-nerdy pirate wear?
An iPatch.

What should you do if you're attacked by a gang of clowns?
Go for the juggler!

What monster eats the fastest?
A goblin!

What planet did the evil aliens crash land on?
Splaturn!

What technique do aliens use for fighting?
Martian arts!

Why do dragons sleep during the day?
So they can fight knights!

Who's the center of attention at a monster dance party?
The boogie man!

What hand should you use to pet King Kong?

Someone else's!

How can you tell if there's a monster under your bed?
Your nose touches the ceiling!

What did Godzilla say after he caused the earthquake?
"Sorry, my fault!"

What do sea monsters like to eat?
Fish and ships!

Why did the headless horseman go to college?
He wanted to get *a head* in life!

Why did the monster's grandma knit him a new sock?
She heard that he grew another foot!

How do you mend a broken jack-o'-lantern?
With a pumpkin patch!

Why did King Kong climb the Empire State Building?

He was too big to use the stairs!

What do you call a one-eyed monster on a motorbike?
A Cycle-ops!

How can I contact the
Loch Ness monster?

Drop it a line!

What monster is gray, has a long trunk, and wears a mask?

The Elephantom of the Opera!

Why is a graveyard a great place to write a book?
It's full of plots!

Where does the yeti keep his money?
In a snow bank.

What would you say if you saw three Cyclopes in a dark alley?
"Eye, eye, eye!"

Did you hear about the monster who was a
Star Trek fan?
**He had one right ear, one left ear,
and one final front-ear!**

Why are ghost kids so happy at the end of the week?
It's Fright Day!

What happened when the vampire bit the cupcake?
She got frostingbite!

What do ghosts use to wash their hair?
Shamboo.

Why did the scarecrow win the Nobel Prize?
He was outstanding in his field!

Who is the scariest singer on the planet?
The Grim Rapper.

That was
a horrible
mummy joke!

I'll say.
It sphinx!

Why did it take so long for Godzilla to gobble up the tower of Big Ben?
It was time-consuming!

What do you call a hairy monster flying a helicopter?
A whirr-wolf!

Why did the zombie get a massage?
She was a little stiff!

SHAGGY: Poor Scooby! The police put him in jail after he ran away from the slime monster.
FRED: Why?
SHAGGY: **He was arrested for leaving the scene of the grime!**

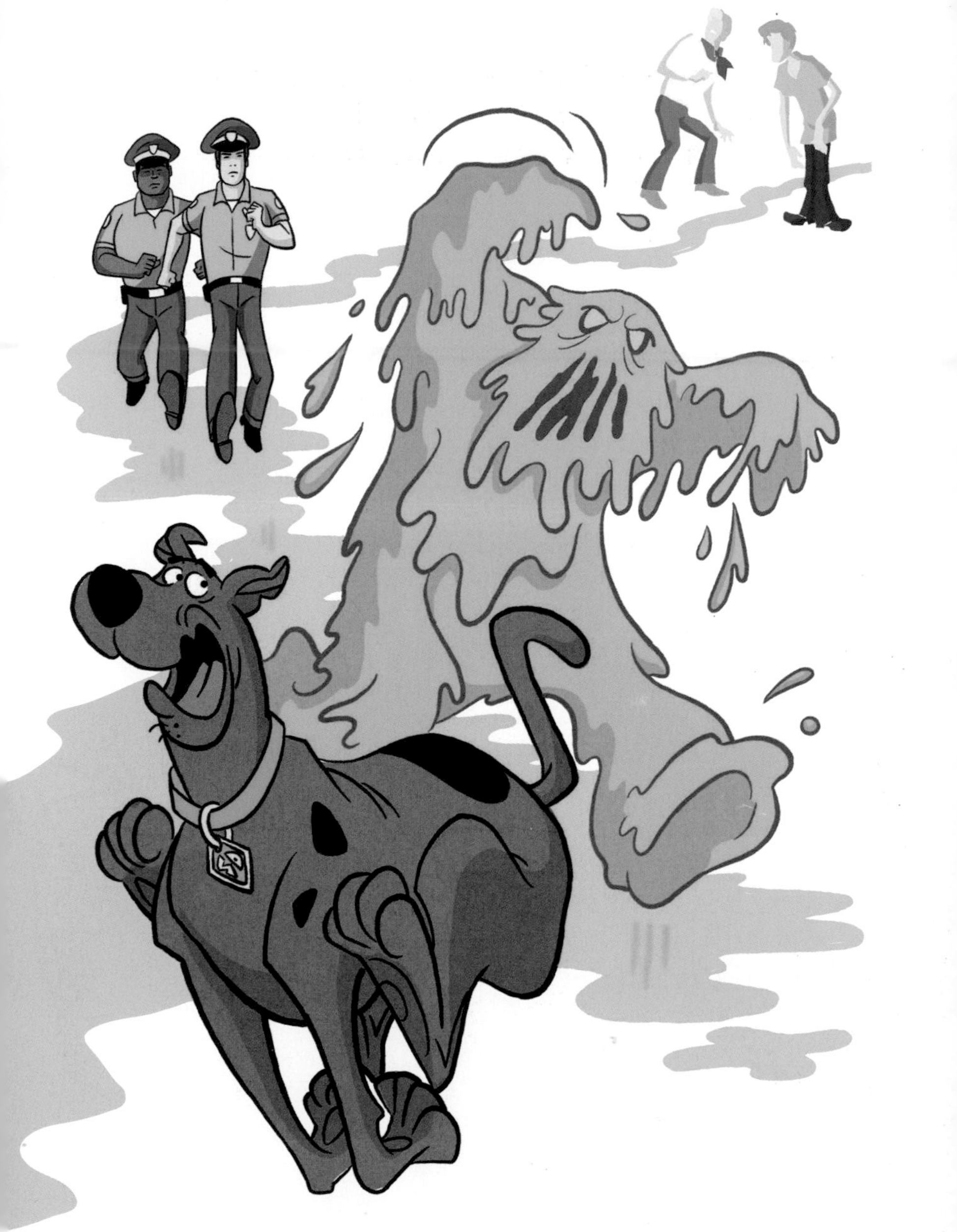

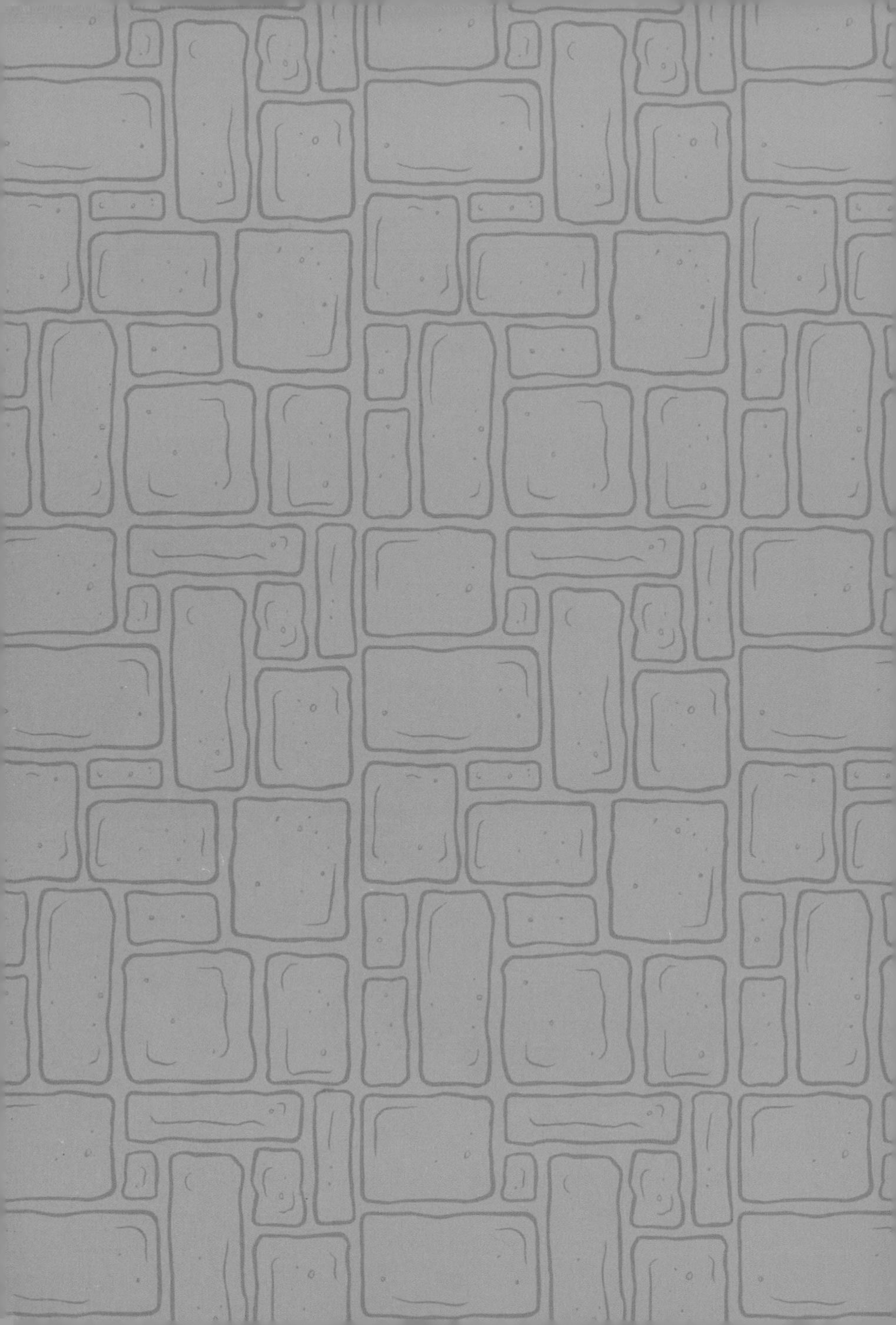

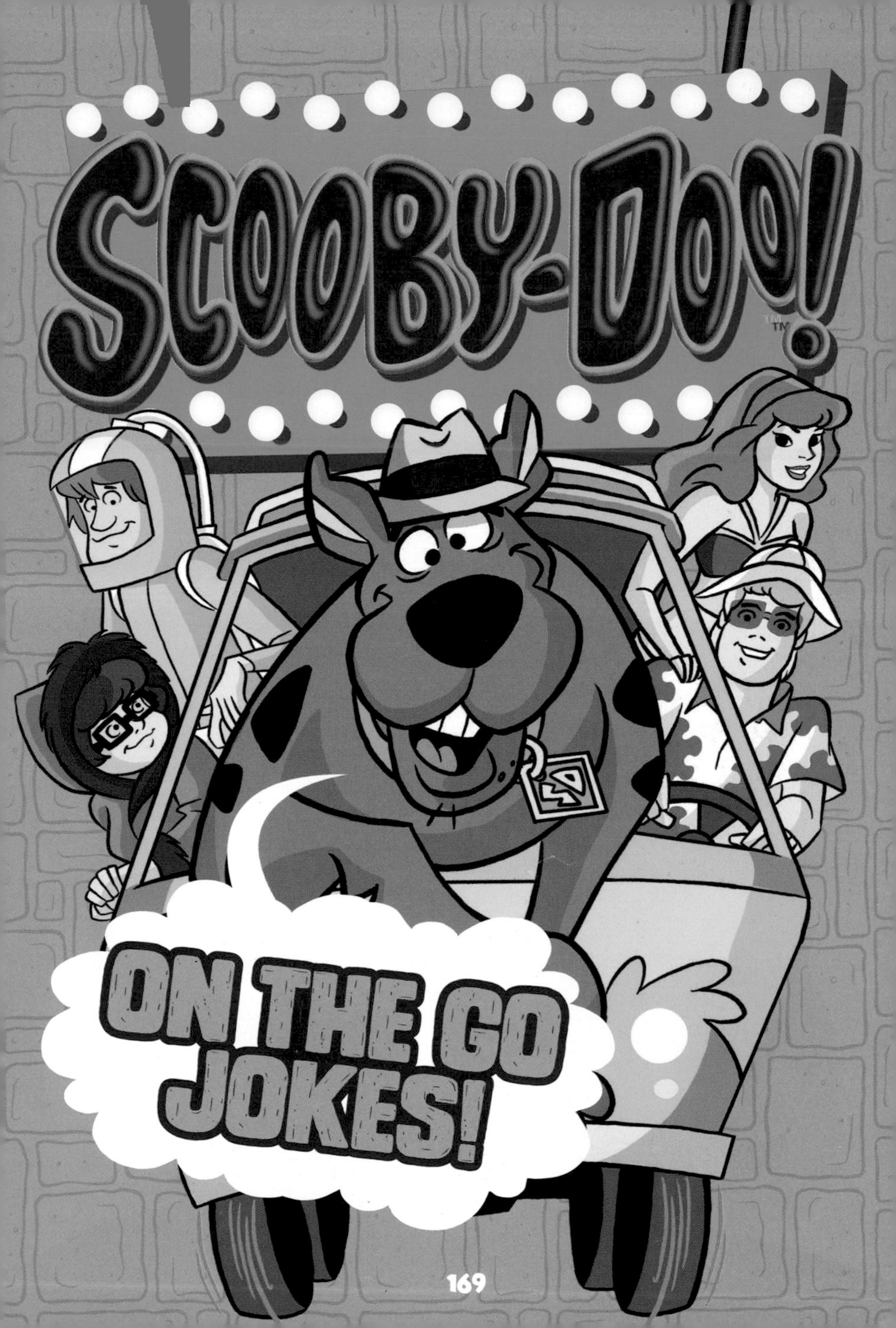
SCOOBY-DOO!
ON THE GO JOKES!

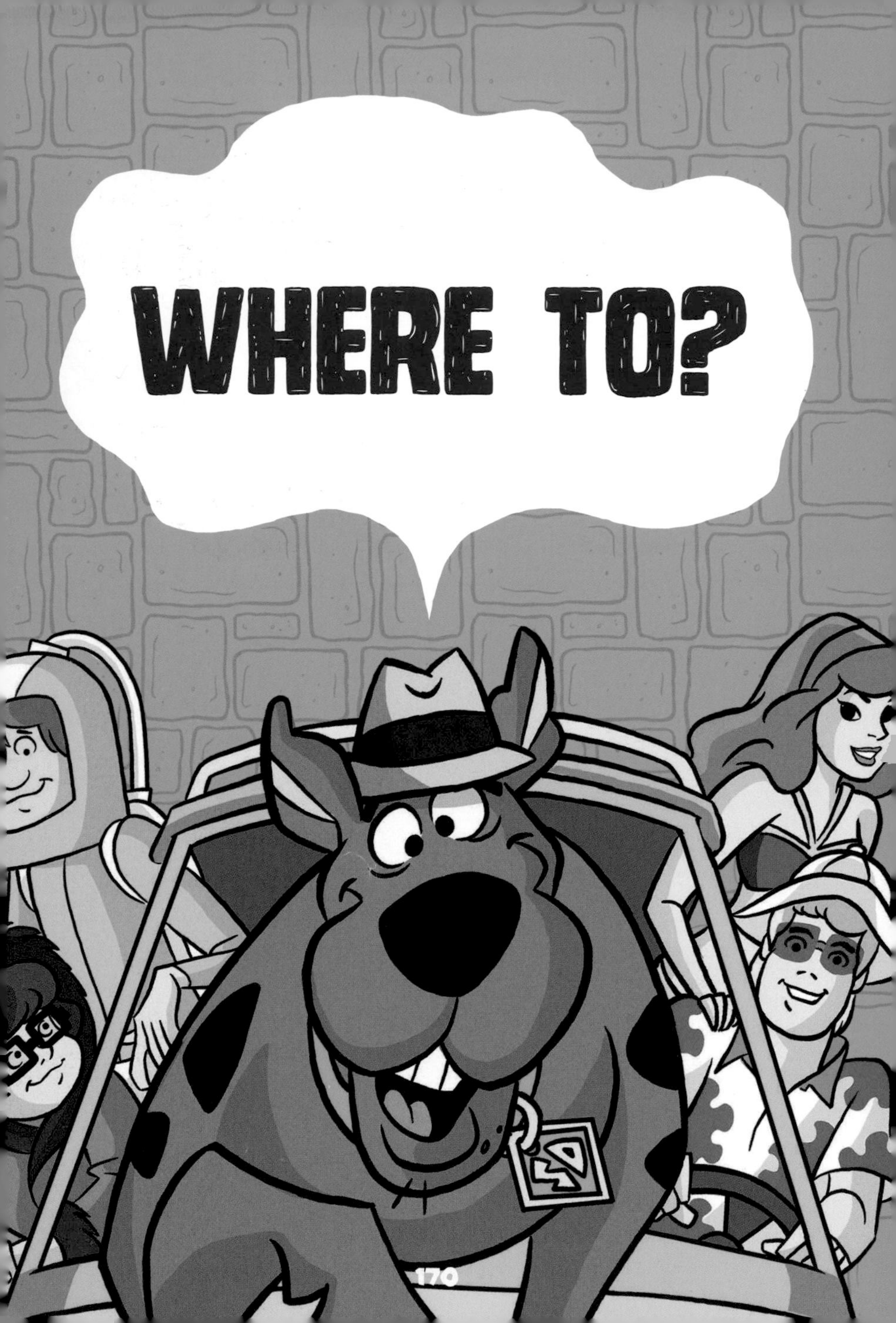
WHERE TO?

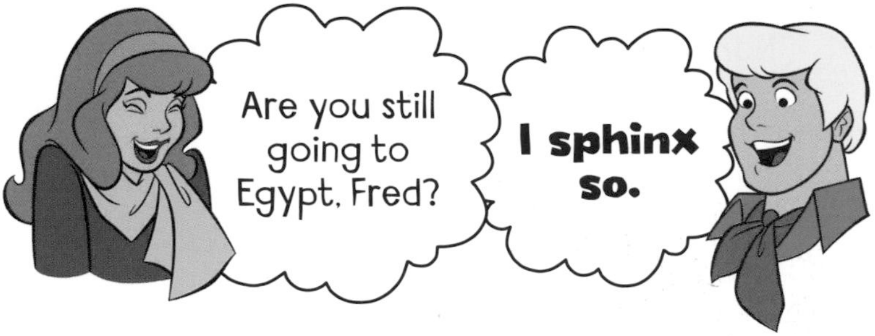
Are you still going to Egypt, Fred?
I sphinx so.

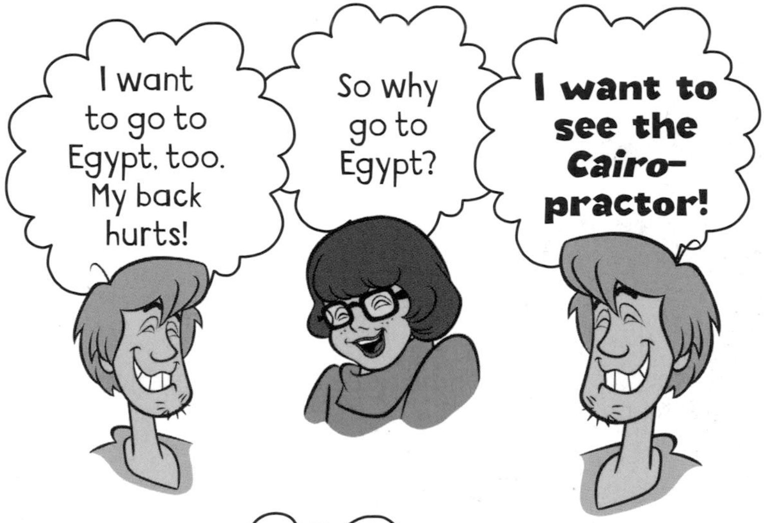
I want to go to Egypt, too. My back hurts!
So why go to Egypt?
I want to see the Cairo-practor!

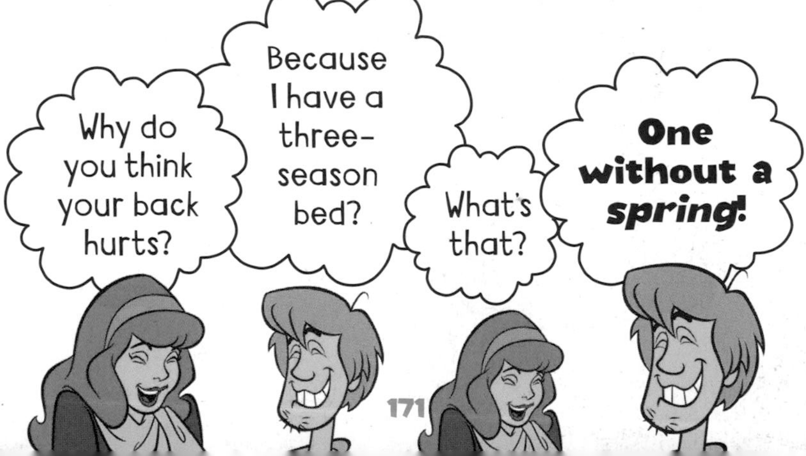
Why do you think your back hurts?
Because I have a three-season bed?
What's that?
One without a spring!

Name a city where there are no people.
Electri City.

What is the smartest country?
Albania. It has three A's and one B!

What European country has the lowest gravity?
No-weigh!

Why did the book go to the psychiatrist?
It kept talking to its shelf!

What do you call a snowman in Florida?
Water.

I hear Scooby might go to college.
Yes, he got a dog *collar*ship!

What is the coldest country in the world?
Chile.

LITTLE GIRL: I'd like to buy a plane ticket for Erwood.
TRAVEL AGENT: Erwood? Sorry, never heard of that. Where is Erwood?
LITTLE GIRL: He's over there. He's my brother.

Sorry, I can't go to the dance. I sprained my ankle.
That's a *lame* excuse!

What do you call a giraffe at the North Pole?

Lost.

What stays in one corner but travels
around the world?
A stamp!

What do you call fear of the North Pole?
Santa Claus-trophobia.

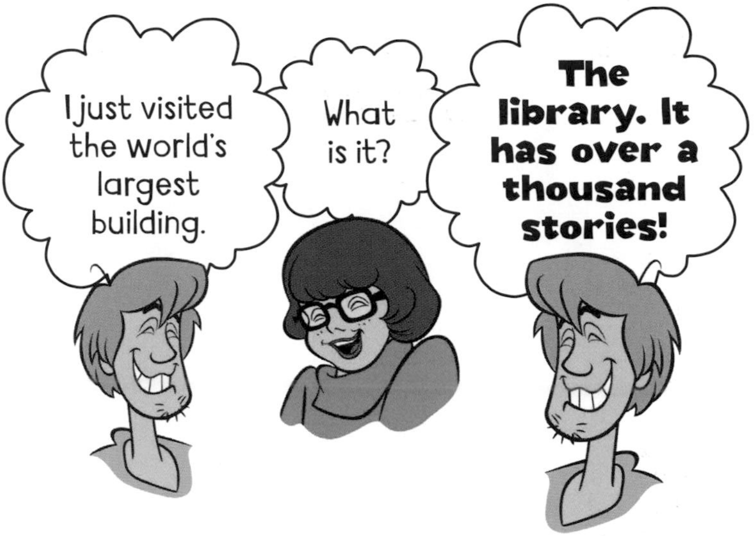
I just visited the world's largest building.
What is it?
The library. It has over a thousand stories!

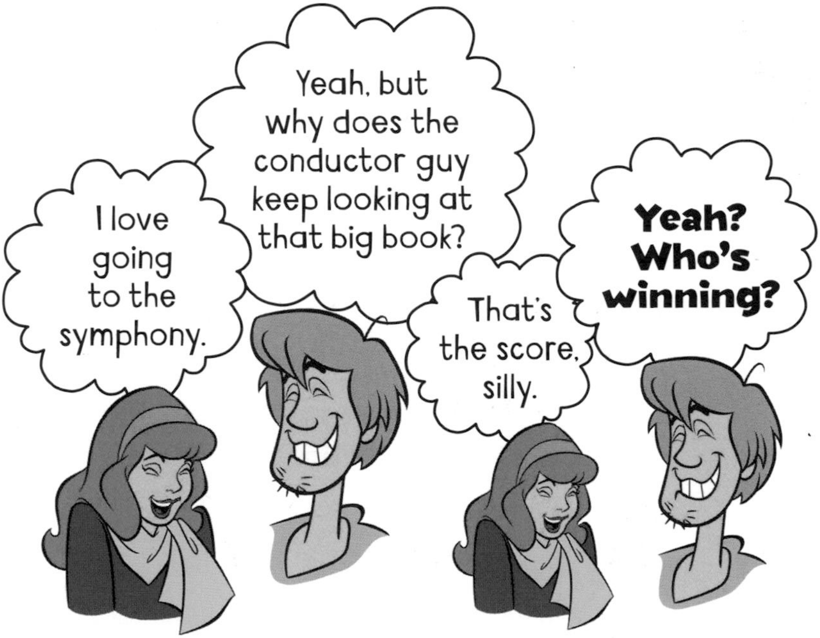
I love going to the symphony.
Yeah, but why does the conductor guy keep looking at that big book?
That's the score, silly.
Yeah? Who's winning?

HIT THE GROUND RUNNING

178

What should you always drink before a race?
Running water!

Did you hear about the runner who was afraid of hurdles?
He got over it.

Why did they throw Cinderella off the basketball team?
She kept running away from the ball!

Marathon runners can race for miles, and they only have to move **two feet!**

Why is the Mystery Inc. gang always so tired on April 1st?

Because they just finished a march of 31 days!

A sloth went out for a walk and was mugged by a gang of snails. When he gave his report to the police, the officer asked, "Can you describe the snails that attacked you?" The sloth said, **"Sorry, it all happened so fast!"**

What does the winner of a race lose?
Her breath.

Did you hear about the two silkworms who had a race?
It ended in a tie.

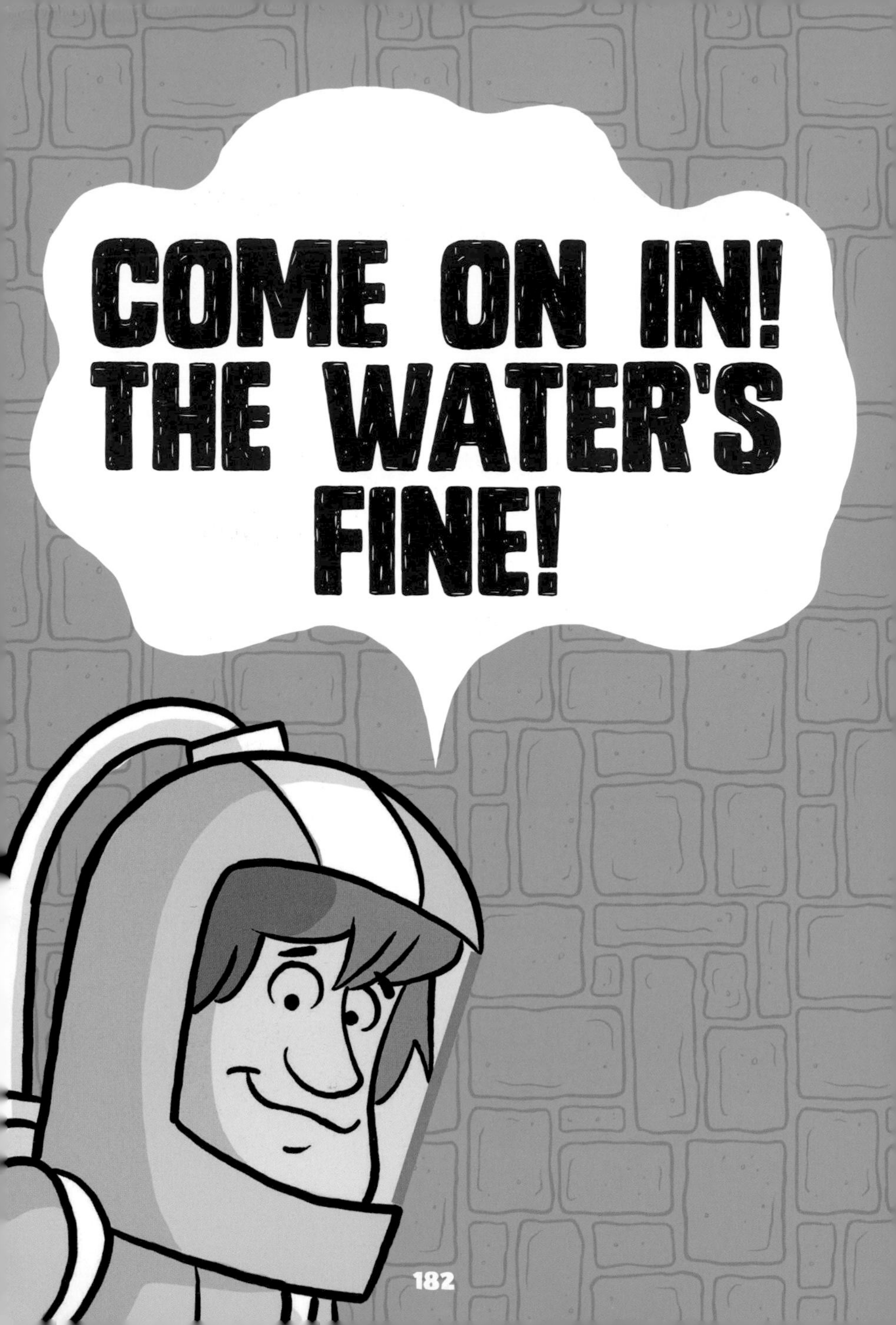
COME ON IN! THE WATER'S FINE!

What do you call little rivers in Egypt?
Juve-niles.

What happened when a red ship crashed
into a blue ship?
The crew was *marooned!*

Why does a ferry always have such
crabby people on it?
Because the boat makes them cross!

Where is the English Channel?
**I don't know. My TV doesn't
pick it up!**

What kind of stories are all about harbor boats?
Ferry tales!

How do surfers greet each other?
They wave!

How do surfers clean themselves?
They wash up on shore!

What did Shaggy say to his friend while they were surfing?
"Scooby-Dude!"

Why are pirates called pirates?
Because they arrrrrrr!

Shaggy went to the beach and sat down next to a sunbathing pig. Shaggy said, "Sure is hot." The pig said,
"You got that right.
I'm bacon!"

Is that boat expensive?
No, it's a sale boat.

Where do you find *micro*waves?
On tiny little beaches!

How did the dentist get across the harbor?
He took the
Tooth Ferry!

What's the best day to go to the beach?
Sun-day!

How did the penguin cross the glacier?
He went with the floe.

Do you know where to find the Dead Sea?
Dead? I didn't even know it was sick!

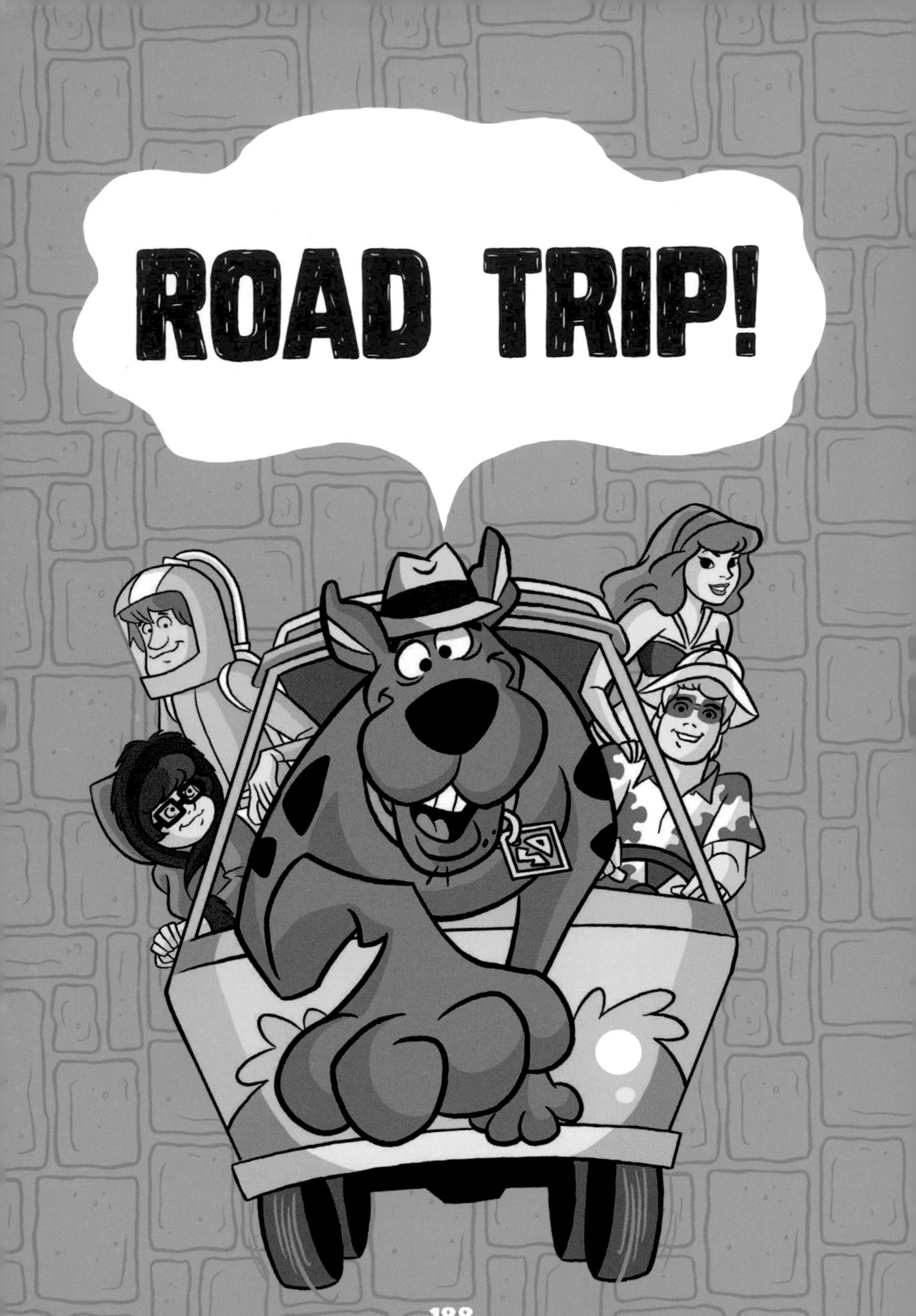
ROAD TRIP!

What has four wheels and flies?
A garbage truck!

Why were you so late to class?
The sign on the street said, "School ahead. Go slow."

What did Dorothy do when her dog got stuck on the yellow brick road?
She called the Toto truck!

Why did the cannibal drive on the highway?
He heard the fast-food stops were serving truck drivers!

I don't think you should ever put a goldfish in a tank.

Everyone knows that fish can't drive!

What driver doesn't need a license?
A screwdriver!

Why don't you see the Mystery Machine parked at football games?
It's not a big van of sports.

Did you hear about the magician who was driving down the road?

He turned into a driveway.

What's worse than raining cats and dogs?

Hailing taxis!

Why does an ambulance always have two medical experts in it?
Because they're a pair-a-medics.

What does a doctor take when she's feeling run down?
The license plate of the car that just hit her!

What happens when a frog parks in a no-parking zone?
It gets toad away!

What kind of vehicle does a mad scientist drive?
A loco-motive!

How does a puppy carry luggage?
Easy, its little tail is a wagon.

Did you hear about the mechanic who slept under the car?

Yeah, he woke up *oily* the next morning.

When does a van stop working?
When it's re-tired.

What do you call a laughing motorcycle?
A Yamahahaha!

What do you get when dinosaurs crash their cars?
Tyrannosaurus wrecks!

When does a van go to sleep?
When it's tired.

What snakes are found on cars?
Windshield vipers!

Who has a job driving customers away?
A taxi driver.

Have you heard the joke about the garbage truck?
Don't worry. It's a load of rubbish.

Why did the Mystery Machine get a hole in its tire?

There was a fork in the road!

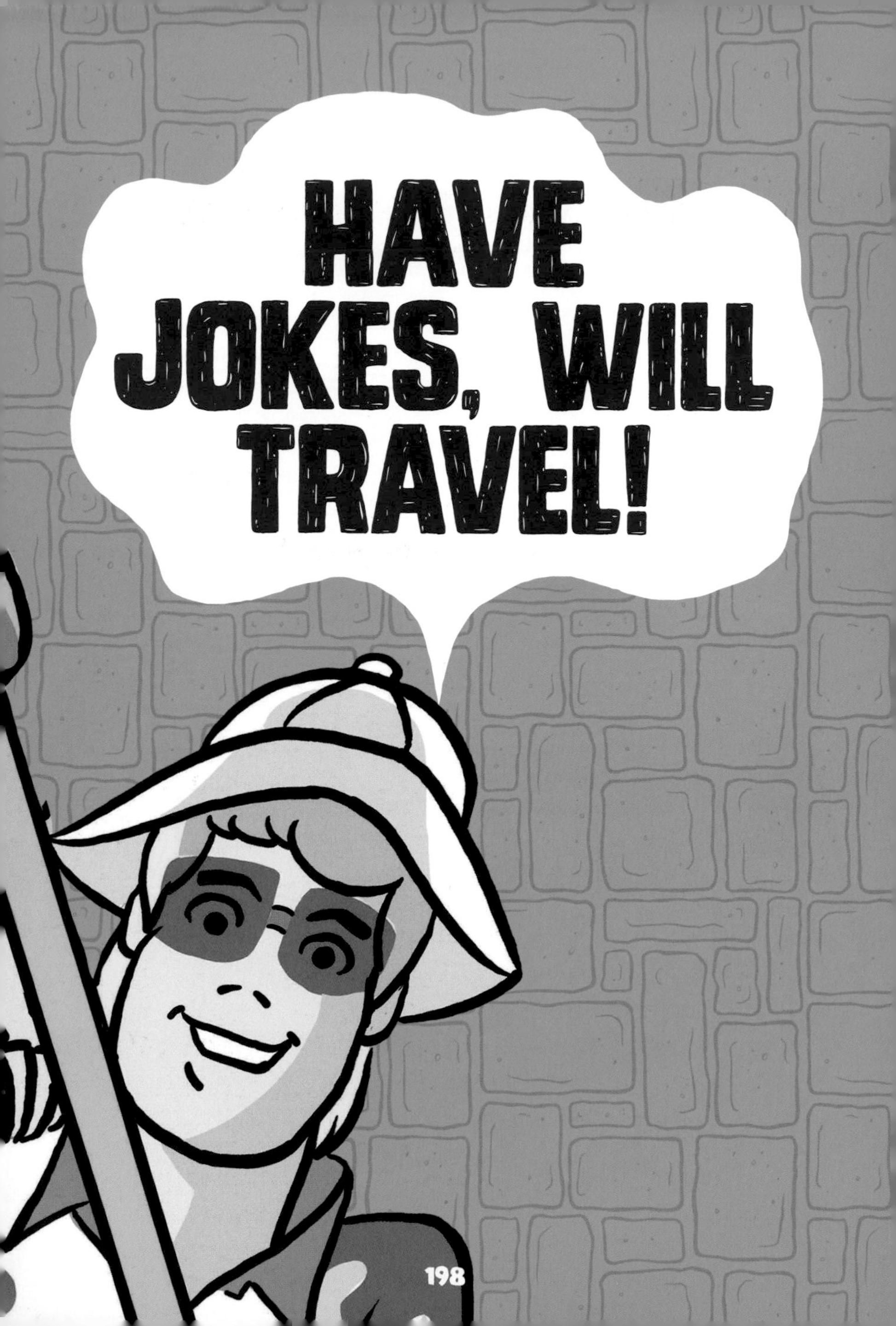
HAVE JOKES, WILL TRAVEL!

What month do soldiers hate the most?
March!

What do you get when you cross a cowboy
with a mapmaker?
A cow-tographer!

What lies on the ground, 100 feet in the air?
A dead centipede.

Shopping is good for helping you see the future!
It helps you see what's in store.

Wow! What a weird-looking painting.
Must be modern art!

**Actually, Shaggy,
that's a mirror.**

Did you hear about the big game hunter who married the telephone operator?

Their lion is always busy!

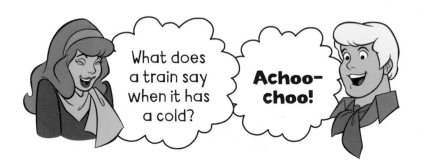

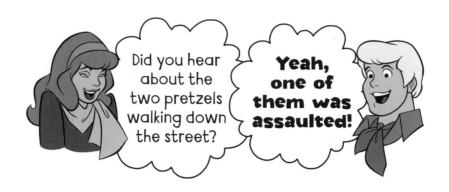

Did you hear about the two pretzels walking down the street?

Yeah, one of them was assaulted!

How do trains hear?
Through their engine-ears!

What's the difference between a teacher and a train conductor?
One trains the mind, and the other minds the train.

What is the difference between a well-dressed man on a tricycle and a poorly dressed man on a bicycle?
Attire!

KID: Doc, my dog thinks he's an elevator!
DOCTOR: Then send him up to see me.

KID: I can't. He doesn't stop at your floor!

How do fleas travel from place to place?

They itch-hike!

Shaggy, what do you have those two hair-curlers
and two butter knives for?

I thought I'd make
some roller-blades!

Why is it good to always travel with a barber?
They know all the short cuts!

Did you hear that Scooby fell into the upholstery machine?
Don't worry, he's fully re-covered!

Did you hear about the fire at the circus?
The heat was in tents!

Why can't the train play music?
It's on the wrong track.

I love staying at the hotel.

If you love it so much, why don't you Marriott?

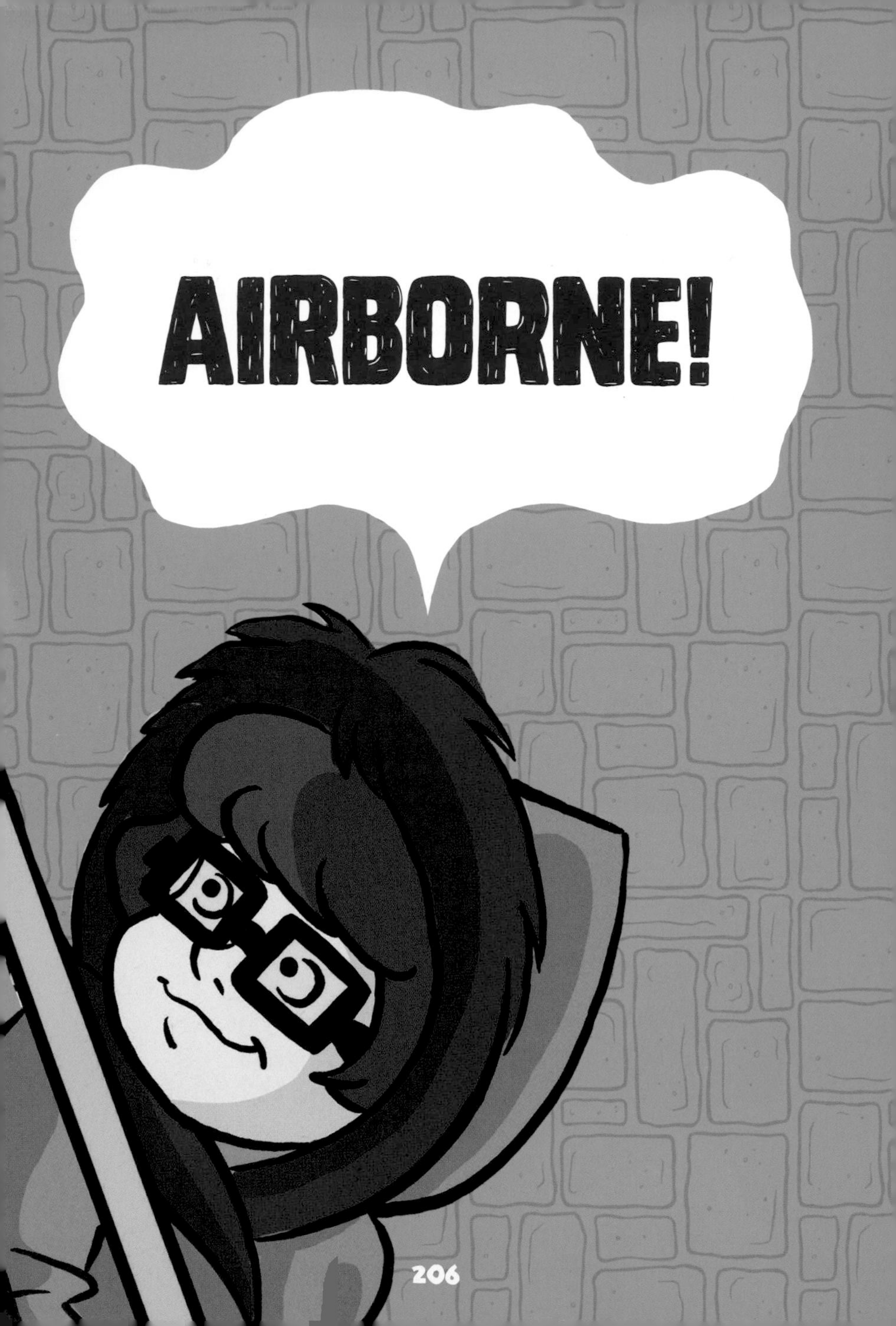
AIRBORNE!

What's the hardest part of skydiving?
The ground.

Why could the vulture only take two
dead raccoons with him on the plane?
**Because they were
considered *carrion* items.**

What only starts to work after it's fired?
A rocket!

Why did the police officer give the balloon a ticket?

It broke the law of gravity.

What happens when you throw a clock in the air?
Time's up!

Scooby wondered why the boomerang kept getting bigger **until it finally hit him!**

What do you get if you cross a dog and an airplane?
A jet setter!

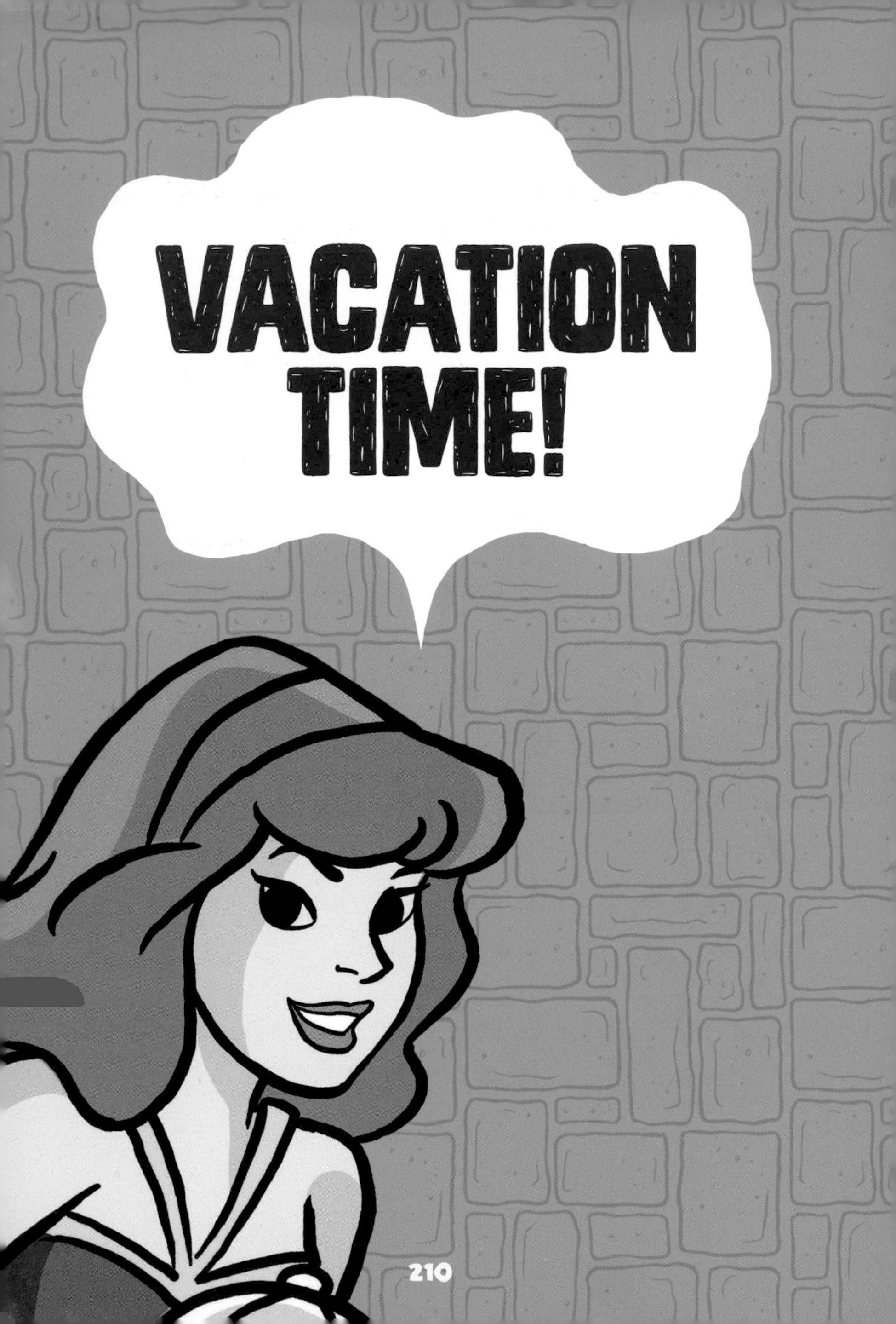
VACATION TIME!

Where did the locksmith go on vacation?
The Florida Keys.

Where did the buffalo go on vacation?
Rome.

Where did the shark go on vacation?
Finland.

Where did the bacteria go on vacation?
Germany.

Where do lumps of sugar go on vacation?
Sweeten!

Where did the knot go on vacation?
Tie-land.

Why did the boxer have a terrible vacation?
All he packed was a punch!

Where did the worm go on vacation?
The Big Apple.

What do you call a piece of paper that
doesn't go anywhere?
Stationary stationery.

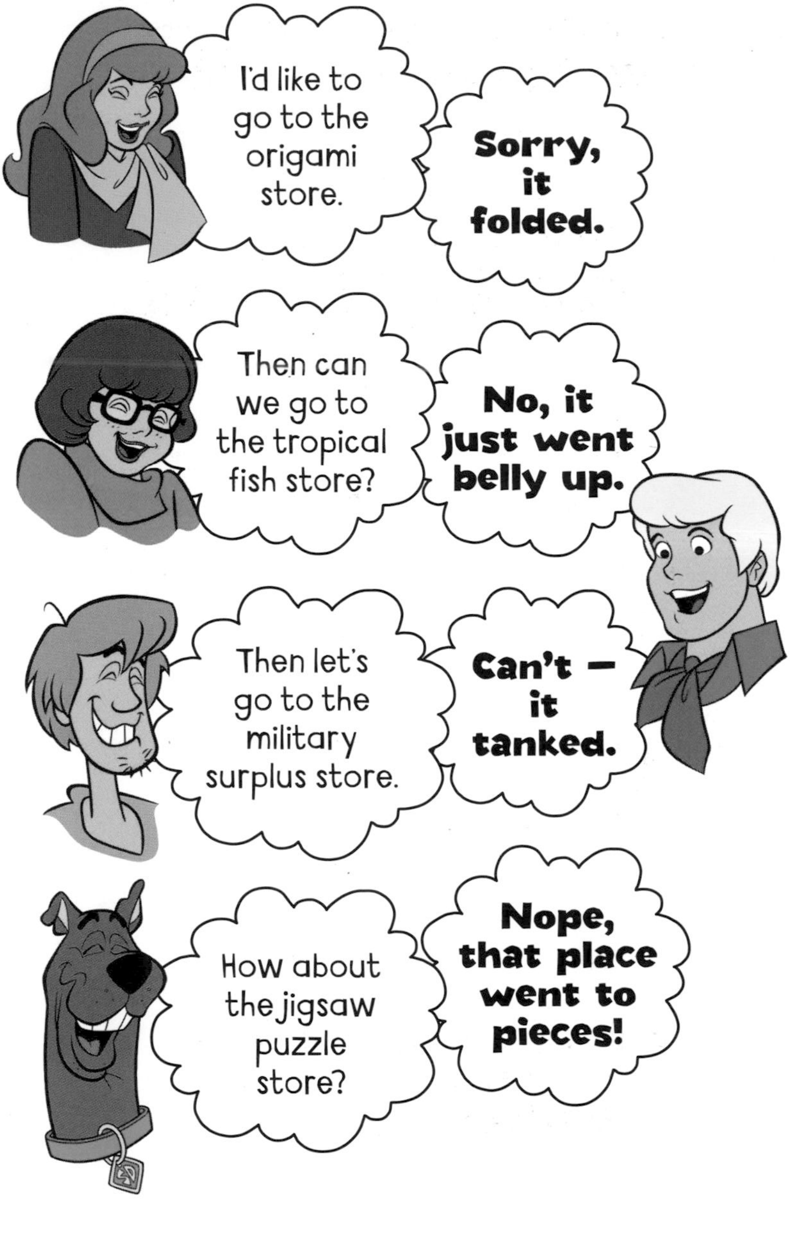
I'd like to go to the origami store.
Sorry, it folded.
Then can we go to the tropical fish store?
No, it just went belly up.
Then let's go to the military surplus store.
Can't — it tanked.
How about the jigsaw puzzle store?
Nope, that place went to pieces!

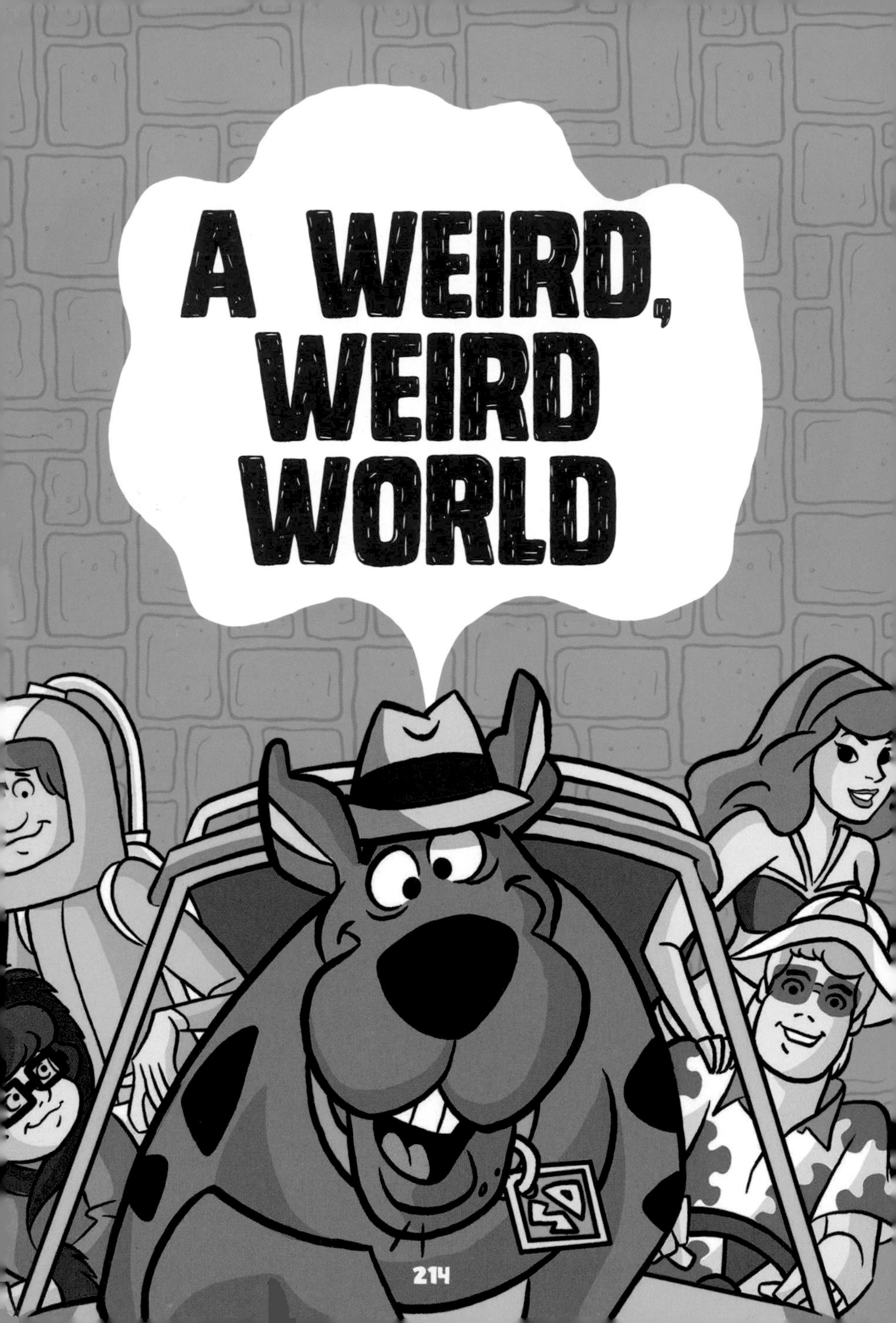
A WEIRD,
WEIRD
WORLD

What is the world's laziest mountain?
Everest.

What is the thirstiest body of water in the world?
The Gulp of Mexico!

Where can you find the Great Plains?
At great airports!

What is the fastest country in the world?
Russia.

Why is the Equator boiling mad?
Because it's 360 degrees!

What stands in New York, holds a torch, and sneezes?
The *Atchoo!* of Liberty.

What's a light-year?
The same as a regular year, but with fewer calories.

What is the wettest country
in the world?

**England.
The queen has
reigned there
for years!**

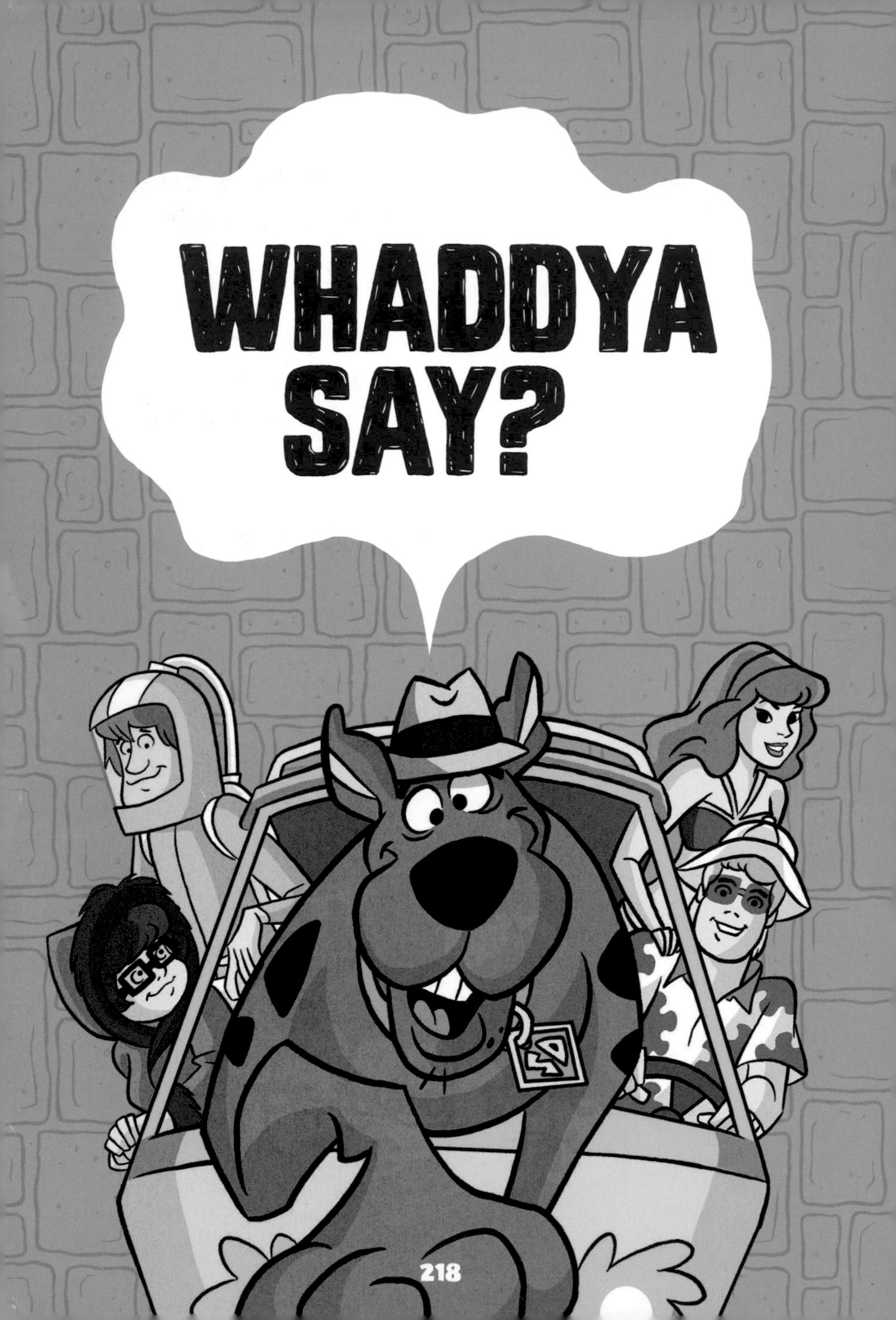
WHADDYA SAY?

What did one elevator operator say to the other?
"I think I'm *coming down* with something."

What did the knapsack say to the hat?
"You go on ahead, I'll go on back."

What did the cowboy say after he was thrown off his horse?
"I've fallen and I can't giddy-up!"

What did the tornado say to the sports car?
"Want to go for a spin?"

What did the jack say to the car?
"Can I give you a lift?"

What did one stoplight say to the other stoplight?
"Don't look! I'm changing!"

What did the rock say to the geologist?

I don't know.

"Don't take me for granite!"

What do you say to a cow that crosses in front of your car?
"Mooo-ve over!"

What did the sleeping bag say to the Boy Scout?
"I've got you covered!"

What did the toadstool say when it moved into its new house?
"Not mushroom in here!"

What did one volcano say to the other?
"I lava you!"

What do you say to a frog who needs a ride?
"Hop in!"

HOW TO TELL JOKES!

1. KNOW the joke.
Make sure you remember the whole joke before you tell it. This sounds like a no-brainer, but most of us have known someone who says, "Oh, this is so funny . . ." Then, when they tell the joke, they can't remember the end. And that's the whole point of a joke — its punch line.

2. SPEAK CLEARLY.
Don't mumble: don't speak too fast or too slow. Just speak like you normally do. You don't have to use a different voice or accent or sound like someone else. (UNLESS that's part of the joke!)

3. LOOK at your audience.
Good eye contact with your listeners will grab their attention.

4. DON'T WORRY about gestures or how to stand or sit when you tell your joke. Remember, telling a joke is basically talking.

5. DON'T LAUGH at your own joke.
Yeah, yeah, I know some comedians break up while they're acting in a sketch or telling a story, but the best rule to follow is not to laugh. If you start to laugh, you might lose the rhythm of your joke or keep yourself from telling the joke clearly. Let your audience laugh. That's their job. Your job is to be the funny one.

6. THE PUNCH LINE is the most important part of the joke.
It's the climax, the payoff, the main event. A good joke can sound even better if you pause for just a second or two before you deliver the punch line. That tiny pause will make your audience mentally sit up and hold their breath, eager to hear what's coming next.